*To Make
Death Love Us*

To Make
Death Love Us

SOVEREIGN FALCONER

DOUBLEDAY & COMPANY, INC.

GARDEN CITY, NEW YORK

1987

All of the characters in this book
are fictitious, and any resemblance
to actual persons, living or dead,
is purely coincidental.

Library of Congress Cataloging-in-Publication Data

Falconer, Sovereign.
To make death love us.

I. Title.
PS3569.T6935T6 1987   813'.54   87–450
ISBN: 0-385-17628-7

To Edgar Allan Poe
and the Knight
in the lighthouse
and to Pat Lobrutto
who has a heart as
big as Maxwell Perkins.
Thank you, Jennie Langdon
You've done an absolutely smashing
copyediting job! Consider yourself
hugged from afar.

*To Make
Death Love Us*

He killed her because she was naked.

It was innocent murder.

The deaf-mute Strong Man slept under the huge truck that transported the traveling sideshow. He'd seen the girl before only hours ago in the company of two men. They had been quite some distance away when his eyes discovered them. Even at that distance, Marco could tell by the way the girl moved rather aimlessly around the two men lounging against the side of their pickup truck, that something was seriously wrong with her.

There was something vaguely familiar about that girl, too. Marco's brow wrinkled with thought as he struggled to remember. He suspected it had something to do with Will Carney and if so, perhaps it meant trouble.

The girl made strange, birdlike gestures, almost hopping around in a human parody of some bird-mating ritual. She had to be either mentally retarded or insane, thought Marco. The Strong Man being unable to either hear or speak, and her lips too far away for him to read, heard none of the things she yelled at the men. But from the way she carried herself, even at that distance Marco knew something was terribly wrong with her. It made him uneasy.

Suddenly, she lifted up her dress, pulling it up to her face. One of the men moved next to her, grabbed the dress, pulled it back in place with a jerk, and then slapped her across the face with such force that she nearly fell. She cowered at his feet like a disciplined dog.

The Strong Man shuddered. He withdrew back inside his tent. The cruelty of the world—ugly, unkind, and all too human—oppressed him.

He sat down on the bench before his barbells and weights. All the tents of the other members of the troupe were down and put away in the truck. Marco knew he should tear down his tent, too, because dawn was not far off and they had to be traveling when the sun came up if they were to make the next stop on time, but he was suddenly too weary. It had been a long day and he thought to sleep in the tent where he could stretch his huge bulk comfortably out at length. The narrow confines of the inside of the truck made him a little claustrophobic, though the other freaks seemed to find it a cozy enough nest.

The flap to his tent was thrust aside and the girl came in, somewhat hesitantly. She stared at Marco, at his thick muscular arms and huge chest.

There was madness in her eyes and manner. Marco sighed and rose slowly to his feet. She stared at his well-developed body with an intensity he found alarming. Marco, who had long ceased to be bothered by the stares of onlookers, got nervous.

Her two brothers, faces red with drink, burst into the tent behind her. That they were her brothers was immediately obvious; there was no mistaking the family resemblance, the same dark eyes, stark features.

She spoke, or rather ranted.

Marco looked away from her face, away from her lips so as not to hear her with his eyes. Madness made him very uneasy.

The two brothers caught her by the arms and rather roughly dragged her out of the tent. Marco did nothing to interfere with her removal. The ease with which they took her bespoke of long custom. Marco, curious, walked to the entrance of the tent and watched her being carried off. They did not take her far.

Across the road only, to a battered white pickup truck with two rifles mounted in a rack inside the cab in front of the back window.

The two brothers let down the tailgate and unceremoniously dumped her on the bed of the truck. They seemed to be threatening her. At any rate, the girl cowered, withdrawing to one corner.

The men dragged a couple of bedrolls out of the truck's cab and pitched them on the ground.

It was obvious they planned to spend the night here, too. Marco shrugged. It did not concern him, although plainly the madness of the girl had upset him. He assumed her two brothers worked as set-up men, ride assemblers for the second-rate carnival the sideshow had temporarily joined forces with.

Marco flexed his muscles uneasily, again withdrawing back inside the tent, closing the flap behind him. The show was done for the day, everything packed away but his tent.

It was hot. Stifling in the tent. Marco lay for hours on a narrow folding cot, adjusting his bulk uncomfortably, sweat dripping from him. Without knowing why, the little episode with the mad girl had upset him. There was a wrongness somewhere, a hint of some impending doom.

The sun was long since down and Marco should be asleep but try as he might he could not get comfortable. The coming of night seemed to oppress him. Sleep eluded him. The other freaks in the sideshow had long since retired for the night. Marco gathered up his blankets and crawled under the huge truck in which the rest of the freaks slept. There was something comforting in the presence of the huge vehicle which was his home, of sorts, as it was for the other freaks in Will Carney's traveling sideshow. Besides, it was much cooler out here. Finally, it seemed sleep found him.

In the dark of the Southern night, a pair of strange eyes watched him as he slept.

The truck was a big old International, the kind used for hauling furniture interstate. It wasn't the biggest of them but it was big enough for the sideshow's purposes. The cab and engine were a part of the whole rig and not separate like the new ones are.

There was a crawlspace behind the driver's seat where a partner could sleep on overnight runs, and a window above that. The window was there so movers could look back through to see if the load was riding all right and served no other useful purpose. It couldn't be opened out or slid aside. The glass was sandwiched for safety's sake.

The back was a big, clamshell tailgate that opened up and ramped down. There was a smaller door in it so if anyone had a mind to look around inside they wouldn't have to open up the whole thing.

On top was a ventilator like a mushroom, about as big as a baby's washtub. There were no windows or openings on the sides of the truck. Instead, a big poster was emblazoned on both side panels, declaring the identity and intentions of the people who traveled in her.

Bold letters at the top said: WILL CARNEY'S TRAVELING CAR-NEE-VAL.

The owner's face—Will Carney himself, wearing a straw hat, smiling, his eyes painted to look warm and friendly—took up a good half of the space on the poster. The rest of it was given over to highly colored representations of the rest of his troupe and what they were about.

Paulette the "HUMAN PACHYDERM," also billed for the less schooled as the "FAT GIRL." Pepino the "RUB-

BER MAN." Colonel John Thumb (he wanted to be billed as a general but everybody agreed that if he was going to borrow the fame of P.T. Barnum's celebrated midget, he'd best be a lot more subtle about it). Marco the "SILENT SAMSON"—who now lay under the truck beginning a dream that would end in murder—and lastly, the oddest of all the freaks, beautiful Serena "THE MOON GIRL," an albino with skin like milk, hair like weed floss, blind eyes, and a strange power within her that grew with each passing day.

The poster had been done by a cut-rate sign painter and was no work of art. It was scaling and peeling off in places so that their faces looked leprous. Some underpainting showed through in spots. If somebody had the mind to look real close, they could see that once the figure of Will Carney, the owner, had had a hand that juggled six red balls and a legend that billed him as WILL CARNEY, THE GREATEST JUGGLER IN THE SOUTH. Rare modesty.

Someone had crudely painted out the hand and the legend with paint that did not match the rest of the poster.

Marco was having a dream. He saw the mad girl coming toward him on all fours. The moon was up, full and huge in the sky like an obscene cue ball and he could see her clearly. She was quite mad. It was clear now.

Mad and naked. Her small, child's breasts were wholly revealed, held high as if in offering. She crawled in under the truck after him. Her eyes rolled wildly in her head and her lips contorted soundlessly, the cords in her throat bulging with effort.

He supposed in the dream that she was screaming at him. Even in the dream there was no sound. Marco lay under the truck, watching her coming up on him like a wild animal stalking its prey and he knew he would wake up before she reached him, for that was the way of dreams. Her hands touched him, caressing his mighty chest. For a dream it was terribly real.

It was such a surprise, such a shock, that Marco reacted before he could think. His huge hands went against her naked body and he shoved her away with all the strength in his corded arms. It was her nakedness that frightened him the most. It made her madness all the more intolerable.

The night itself was alive with noise, but Marco heard none of it. Car doors slammed, men shouted as they stumbled in the dark, cursing, running blindly in the dark toward the source of the screams.

The girl was propelled backward as if thrown by a catapult. Her body smashed, with a sickening thud, into a utility pole a full fifteen feet from the back of the truck. Her head snapped back and she slumped in a heap at the base of the pole. Blood spurted from her mouth and ears and her head lolled sideways at an unnatural angle. Her neck had snapped like a twig. For a dream, Marco found it all to be sickeningly real. He stirred, shuddered, waiting for the moment that would shake him out of this nightmare.

A face seemed to hover over him, intruding in this strange dream. It belonged to Will Carney, the owner of the sideshow. He seemed to be shouting at Marco. An arm and hand reached out for him. As part of the dream, it had no meaning to Marco.

Will shook his shoulder roughly. In the distance, someone turned their headlights on, and Marco could see the mad girl's two brothers standing in the headlight's glare beside their pickup truck. They were screaming, although Marco could not hear it. As one, they raced to the cab of their pickup and yanked the rifles out of the rack in the back window. It all seemed very real, this nightmare.

Will seemed to have Marco very firmly by the shoulder now, dragging him out from under the truck—no mean feat in itself, considering Marco's weight. No part of the dream faded. The girl still lay by the pole like a broken doll.

Marco stumbled clumsily alongside Will in the dark. He decided then to wake up, to open his eyes and abolish this dream, but in this Marco failed. He found with a shock that his eyes had been open all along and that this was no dream.

It was real.

It had all happened.

At Will Carney's frantic urging, Marco steadied himself and ran with Will toward the cab of the truck. A shot rang out and something fierce and hot and heavy stung Marco in the shoulder. Marco did not hear it, only felt it tearing through him. Will screamed and practically heaved Marco bodily up into the cab. Marco reached back with one hand and gathered up Will Carney, heaving him across his lap as if Will were no heavier than spun cotton, plunking Will down behind the steering wheel.

To Marco it was all still like a dream but his head was clear and his huge body was quick to respond.

The starter ground and the diesel engines jumped reluctantly into life. Marco turned his head, looking down at his shoulder. A bullet had entered it from the back and gone completely through. Blood dripped down his massive arm, staining his pants.

Will slammed the truck into gear and they jumped forward to the accompaniment of screams from the freaks inside the van of the truck. A dark figure leaped up on the running board and a rifle barrel smashed through the window. Marco reacted with a quickness that belied his size. He seized the gun barrel with both hands and twisted it into a U shape. The gun went off, exploding into fragments. Pieces of metal shattered the lower-right-hand corner of the windshield. Several pieces of gun metal struck Marco in the chest and legs. The man who had fired the gun was thrown off the running board by the blast.

Will Carney pushed the accelerator to the floor and the truck careened down the midway, tires squealing in protest. They weaved dangerously from side to side, down the narrow concourse. The rear end of the truck snagged an edge of canvas and a half-erected shooting gallery collapsed into the basketball-throw concession.

Marco shook his head. It had all happened so fast. He stared at the ragged hole in his shoulder. The gunshot wound was real enough. The girl, too. He'd killed her. Quite by accident but true all the same. His great strength had betrayed him. Funny he should have thought it all a dream. Marco almost never dreamed. Dreams took more imagination than Marco had.

Will Carney had no time to think, to plot his course. Flight had been his instinctive reaction to trouble. Had he been thinking, he would have abandoned Marco, left him to face the trouble by himself, but Will had been caught unprepared. Even now, Will's mind considered the possibility of stopping the truck, of shoving Marco out to face the music. Will Carney's mind was not one that put great store in loyalty.

Will's eyes were on the rearview mirror when the headlights came into view. He expected it, of course. They came up very fast behind him. He had the accelerator to the floor but the big truck was not exactly a racing car.

In the back of the truck, the freaks tumbled about like feathers in a storm.

The white pickup gained on them. Will cursed and swerved to the middle of the narrow road, preventing them from passing. There was a spurt of flame from the pursuing truck and Will's outside mirror disintegrated.

"Oh sweet Jesus!" he said. The road angled, dipping into a deep curve. Will took the curve too high and in the middle realized that he would not make it. He had no time to even cry out.

Will's eyes caught something brown and flat in the glare of the headlights, something dividing the heavy brush at the top of the curve. Instinctively, Will ducked down behind the wheel, bracing himself for the inevitable crash.

Marco's huge hand came out and seized the wheel. With a mighty yank, he hurled the truck to the right, toward the narrow dirt road branching off from the top of the curve. It was an impossible turn for a truck that size and at that speed but, somehow, the truck lurched sickenly, bucked, sawfished as it went off the road, and then tailed out and—guided by the strong hand of Marco—found the bed of the rutted lane and plunged down it. The road seemed to go straight down.

It was a logging road, rutted and gutted and not used since the turn of the century. The truck thundered down the mountain road like a storm-maddened bronco.

The pickup truck went past the turnoff, brakes locked, tires squealing. It stopped, spun around completely in the road, stalled out. It started up again immediately, roared back toward the cutoff, turned, and plunged down the old logging route after them.

Will rose back up, knocking aside Marco's huge hand from the steering wheel, taking control of the truck again. He couldn't understand what had kept them on the road. Marco slumped back against the seat. The demand on his strength coupled with the loss of blood was beginning to tell on him. The horror of what had happened was just beginning to sink in.

It washed over Marco in a tidal wave, draining him of all strength. Without meaning to, his huge body had betrayed him, had taken the life of a girl—mad perhaps, but still a human being for all that. His huge body and slow mind clotted with sorrow and shame.

Will had no time for such thoughts, the road down which they plunged twisted and dove and bottomed out in hideously complicated S turns. He had all he could do to keep the truck on the road. The ruts and washouts threatened to rip out the bottom of the truck. His head, time and time again, smashed into the ceiling of the cab as the truck bottomed out. The freaks in back of the truck were screaming in terror but Will Carney had no thoughts for them, only for survival, for Will Carney, for piloting this mad rush down the mountain.

The pickup truck slammed down the mountain after them, rapidly gaining on them as they plunged headlong down the dark North Carolina mountain. Its headlights picked out the huge truck clearly. It rushed down on them. Around one hairpin curve, it came down so fast on them the front bumper caught a piece of the tailgate, almost ramming them on past the turn to crash into the side of a cliff. Somehow, Will Carney kept the truck aligned with the curve.

As if to add to their troubles, a raindrop smashed against the windshield, poking a hole in the dust. Then another and another, huge droplets. Will Carney gripped the wheel as if it were life itself. "My Lord!" he said, as though it were a blasphemy. He was terrified.

The first drops became a host. The driver turned on the wipers. They sang and squeaked across the window with every swipe. The rain tumbled in sheets across the glass. The road, ruined as it was, almost disappeared from sight.

"My Lord!" gasped Will, finding no comfort.

The truck plunged madly down the mountain, on the one side the rock cliffs and, on the driver's side, a sheer drop into nothingness and certain death.

Inside the body of the van, the human attractions

rocked back and forth, thrown violently from their seats, cursing and crying by turns. All the gear and housekeeping goods were with them in that space, lashed down but not so secure that anyone in the back would feel cheerful about it.

Paulette, the Fat Lady, kept her eyes closed, even in the almost dark, because it stilled her fears a bit. Serena's eyes were wide open, seeing absolutely nothing and wishing to God she could so that she wouldn't be so afraid. She could taste death on her tongue, could even smell it in the very air.

The death of the mad girl was not unknown to Serena, nor was silent Marco's part in it. Her mind held a window open to the world her eyes could not see.

Pepino had his arms and legs braced here and there. He looked like a big spider clinging to the center of its web. He was afraid for himself in all the lurching and bumping. A double jointed man is fragile to injury. The Midget, John Thumb, was the curser among them. His swearing did little to chase away his own fears.

The rain came down unmercifully. What dirt there was on the granite face of the mountain ran out from beneath pebbles and rocks, down the fissures of great age, and made the road even more slick and treacherous. Up above the roadway, some distance ahead, the mountain shuddered in the wet and a fall of dirt and small boulders rattled down to the old road.

Some of it spilled cross the road like swallows skating across the sky, and plunged over the edge. The echoes of the rocks falling, were there anyone to hear, would have been a terribly long time coming.

Will Carney rode the brakes with all his strength. They felt spongy and unresponsive. They were beginning to wear thin. Ahead of him, the mountain gave up a piece of itself. A massive slide swept down the face, ripping up a half dozen stunted sugar pines, crashed down on the ruined road and gouged a huge section out of it, tumbling it down to the bottom of the gorge.

Will Carney double-clutched, slammed the stick shift into low gear with his one good hand. His right foot was set halfway from gas to brake. The pickup in back of them smashed into their tailgate again. Will's foot hit the gas pedal, slamming the truck forward, pulling away from the truck ramming them. The lightning flashed and in that brief moment Will saw an emptiness in the dark ahead that wasn't right. His belly told him before his eyes. The yellow wash of the headlights caught the raindrops falling free in space, falling in that way that says there's no ground underneath.

Boulders still spilled down the mountain, careening down past the headlights, plunging into the gorge far below.

Will's foot slammed on the brake pedal. Too hard. The truck's wheels locked. It skidded toward the pit. Will jerked the wheel hard right, toward the huge rock face of the mountain. The big, all-weather tires on the truck fought the rain soaked surface of the road . . . and lost.

Marco's huge body slid across the seat, slamming into Will, pinning him against the driver's door, tearing the steering wheel out of his hands.

The truck hit the mountainside, half tipped, ran a wheel up a slope of earth and rock newly deposited by the slide. The front went out into space. It's weight threw it a good distance as it started to fall over the edge, into the darkness below. A projection of rock slammed into the top of the van, ripping the metal. Somehow, miraculously, the truck caught there, as neatly as an insect pinned to a board.

The cab and two thirds of the body were suspended

over emptiness. The right wheel had purchase on doubtful ground. A delicate balance was keeping her cradled on
the breast of the mountain.

Marco's door was jammed right up against the belly of
the slide with no way to get out.

The pickup truck roared down on them, headlights im-
paling them. Will screamed, awaiting the impact that
would send them over the edge and to certain death.

Serena smiled in the darkness; her mind searched the
night. It found those who pursued and silently, secretly it
dealt with them. Her mind went into their minds and, like
a bright fire, it sent sparks hurtling down the synapse
chains, impulses down into unresisting muscles.

The pickup came screaming down the grade, straight
for them. At the last moment, muscles responded, surged,
and the wheel was wrenched to the left, toward the open
sky and the pickup soared past them off into space.

Will Carney heard them scream as they went over.
Marco, slumped on his shoulder, saw them go down, too,
saw the truck bounce once, like a toy kicked down a long
flight of stairs. Then the truck burst into flame, pinwheel-
ing like a fiery comet down toward the bottom of the
gorge.

Serena, in the darkness of the van, could not see the two
men die but she felt it, none the less. Their screams
seemed to echo within every part of her. Their terror was
a huge lake within her. The flames reached her inside the
truck, a burning; searing pain burned inside her but it was
soon ended. She fainted.

Marco raised himself off of Will, moving back toward his
side of the truck.

The truck shuddered, tilted, seemed to be going over
the edge.

"Jesus Christ! Don't do that!" Will Carney screamed.

There was no need for the warning. Marco sensed the

skittish movements that accompanied his efforts and he slumped into motionlessness.

Inside the dark van there was screaming.

"Don't move back there! Don't you move a quarter of an inch!" Will Carney bellowed as loud as his lungs could make.

There was some silence, a cessation of movement but Paulette's whimpering did not stop.

Marco moved one hand. His movements were slow, exaggerated by the loss of blood, beginning to tell, even on his mighty body. He touched Will's hand and indicated the ignition key. The motor was stalled but the key was still in the "on" position.

"So what?" Will said more in fear than anger. He was in a state of near shock.

Marco pointed to the floor, at the starter pedal. He was clearly telling Will that he might, just accidentally, stomp on it and turn the motor over just enough to kill them all.

Will reached forward—his ears pricked for any grating sound, for any sudden shift in the truck—and switched the key to "off." Then he reached over a bit more and turned the headlamps off. Might as well save the battery.

He eased back into the seat and breathed again in the pitch dark. His body was drenched with sweat, his face as pale as old death. He stared out the shattered windshield.

It was as black as a dead eye on the mountain.

Will Carney's mouth was too dry to make spit. Yet he wanted the harsh smoke of a cigarette more than he could ever remember wanting anything in his life.

Trouble was—he let himself admit it—there had been a million and one things he'd wanted in his life in just that way.

"Let me have just this one thing, God, and I'll never ask for another thing." Now, how many times had he said that?

After he stopped calling on an unhearing God to pop jelly beans into his mouth, he'd thought of a vague anybody to grant his futile and petty wishes. Later still, he'd ask in the name of the "juggler" and that meant that there was no God for Will Carney, no gift givers or treasure makers, only himself, Will Carney, bellied up to the rotten business of living. Naked, alone.

All right. All right-ee.

It's that way, then, and no other.

Will learned to smile and laugh all over his face so that people didn't notice his sharp eyes watching them to see what he could charm them out of. He learned the manner of words like "Ma'm; sir; good Lord; mercy, baby; honey this and honey that; and sweet lover." Words much abused; words that didn't mean much, the way he meant them, had nothing to do with what he was saying inside himself, but which made songs for other people, it seemed.

Will combed his hair in the middle when he was a youth, thinking it made him look a touch old-fashioned and therefore, unthreatening. He treasured the dimple marks at the sides of his mouth. They had earned him a bed and a meal when hard work would not. He admired the set of his own shoulders and padded the jackets of his suits to square them better.

In those overblown suits, he looked somewhat like a turtle, ready at the first sign of danger to pop back in his shell. Even so, he was called, more often than not, good looking. Most people he met never saw past his smile.

He sat in the darkened cab like a puppet with severed strings. He fished a pack of cigarettes out of his shirt pocket and shook one out. He trembled. His muscles pained from doing even that simple thing, so afraid was he that any movement would send them plunging over into the dark, into the death that awaited them all.

Will started to stretch his hand to the cigarette lighter set in the dashboard. He hesitated, afraid to lean forward lest it be his last act. A match flared in the hands of Marco.

Will turned and looked into the man's pain-wracked eyes. He knew the mute had been staring at Will in the blackness. The Strong Man's face was deathly white in the flare of the match. He was still losing blood. Perhaps he would die of it.

The eyes of the silent Strong Man were like two pin points of wondering pain. It was old pain and new pain. Those eyes in the dark reminded Will of someone. Funny at a place like this, at a time like now, he should think of that.

He remembered,

A man named Thorne had come through the county
seat one day when Will Carney was fourteen. The man
sold medicines of a sort, mostly made of alcohol. It was all
right for God-fearing people to have a nip of the demon's
brew, if it tasted of herbs with a vague claim of being
curative and lay bitter as sin itself on the tongue. To draw
a crowd and get the unsophisticated fools thirsty, this man
Thorne entertained them with some fancy juggling.

As the little balls sped around, cutting patterns in the
air, Will prayed that if he could be blessed with the skill of
such a wonder he'd never ask for another thing as long as
he lived. Thorne saw the marvel of his juggling in the
boy's bright eyes, an admiration . . . no . . . adoration
of a quality he'd never seen before, and Thorne found
himself making special play to that round-eyed audience
of one.

When the show was over, the crowd scattered away on
their own business, and Thorne invited the boy to try his
hand. Before the hot afternoon was done, Will, all sweaty
with exertion and cheerful beyond bearing, could keep
three balls in the air at one time with one hand and
scratch himself with the other.

The juggler made much over it and asked after the
boy's relatives and family. There were none. Will Carney
was a ward of the county, in a manner of speaking. And so
Will left that night to join what he believed to be the
wonderful world of carnival and circus.

They camped along the roadways and cooked their
night meal. In the fireglow, the juggler would stare at
young Will sometimes, as he told stories of wonders past
believing. It was then, sometimes, in the middle of some
incredible lie, that the old juggler's eyes would spark with
hate, with a bitterness within himself. Will would close his
eyes, then, so as not to see the darkness in the old man's
eyes.

There came a time, when Will was sixteen, when the hate in the juggler's eyes could not be closed out. The old man came across the fire at Will, with his hands out like hooks meant to grasp and choke. A knife flashed in Will's hands, his first instinctive reaction to sudden attack and without quite meaning to, he impaled the old man on it.

The old man sighed as if he felt the tide going out and fell across Will, one leg dragging in the fire. Will rolled him over, pulling the old man's leg out of the fire, knife slipping from his hand. Will's eyes were wide with surprise, with hurt, with disbelief.

The old man, dying slowly, sighed yet again. "Just not quick enough," he said.

"What the hell got into you!" screamed Will. "Why did you do it?"

The old man said, "You took my woman in Bennet City into your bed. She belonged to me. You shouldn't have done it."

Will was stunned. "I *took* her! Why, you damned old fool, she *took* me into hers. And she didn't belong to you. She was for everybody who had the price and freely said so."

"She was mine," insisted the dying juggler. "You had no right to her."

"She wasn't important, not worth dying for," said Will. "I just wanted to learn about making love. It could have been anybody. It just happened to be her."

"You seduced her," accused the old man. "That isn't right."

"You're crazy. When she wasn't giving it away, she was selling it. At least, that's what everyone said. Didn't you know? You had to know," said Will.

"But I loved her," the old juggler said, and softly began to cry.

"But she was a prostitute," protested Will. "She didn't

belong to you. She didn't even belong to herself. She wasn't ever a purchase, just a rental, as the song says."

But the old man went on, as one deaf. "You knew I saw her as mine, pretend or no. You had no right to her. There were plenty more you could have had as easy." He coughed. Flies gathered in a swarm around the red gash in his chest. The knife had gone in deep.

Will shook his head, as if angry at the flies that had gathered.

The old man's eyes still flashed with anger, with the ages old hatred of man over woman. "You bought her then, with the money I gave you. My money! You had no right."

Will cursed himself, cursed the stubborn old man dying at his feet. He understood the games of life, the risks and sometimes the reasons, the ways to win and to lose. He had some insights into the things men do to "get by." But even at his age, young as he was, the terrible need most men had to tell lies to themselves and then believe them, still amazed him. The old man's illusions that he was loved by a whore who loved none who walked the face of this earth, was a thing past his understanding. It was a blindness he himself might be prone to someday, for he could not understand it in others.

"I never paid her, not with money, anyway. All I did was smile at her. That was all. I swear I never paid her. Never more than a smile. Why did she take me into her bed? Maybe because I had never been with a woman and she knew it. I think she understood that and wanted to cure me of it. Why shouldn't I have gone with her?"

The old man coughed, blood flecking the corners of his lips.

"Because I'm old and getting older. Because of what I taught you about making balls stay up in the air."

"No."

"For friendship, then." The old man was getting weaker.

"No."

"For the love of God."

"No."

"In the name of the juggler, then," said the old man, shuddering, dying with his eyes open.

Will Carney bowed his head, tears streaming down his face.

"Yes. In the name of the juggler," he said.

So that was where the saying had come to him. Will had almost forgotten that.

He dragged the smoke into his lungs. He enjoyed it. Didn't have to worry about dying of lung cancer, since he wasn't going to live through the night. That thought scared him all over again. His insides churned and he had to fight to keep from throwing up.

"Mr. Carney," Paulette shouted from inside the van. "What am I supposed to do? I got to pee so bad."

Maybe some other time Will would have laughed at that but not now.

"Don't you move, goddamn it!" Fear was like a black beast crawling down his throat, attacking his spine. "You just do it right where you're sitting!"

"But I'm wedged in standing up," she cried, obviously distressed.

"I don't care if you're upside down! I say you don't move a goddamn inch and you goddamn well better not!"

Will took another drag on the cigarette and was foolishly cheered by the glow. It was beginning to burn his fingers. He spit into his palm—where the spit came from he wouldn't know—and let the glowing coal sizzle out. It sounded like the hiss of a man's last breath.

"We got to do something," he said to Marco, though he knew the deaf-mute Strong Man couldn't hear a word of it. "This rain will keep washing the dirt and rock away until there's nothing left for the wheels to stand on. What the hell we gonna do? Jesus Christ, it's dark!"

Will turned his head, staring in the dark.

"Wish I knew what you were thinking. Sitting there bleeding in the dark. You bastard! I suppose you blame it all on me. I bet you're staring hate through me. I'll bet you can see in the dark, too, you freak son of a bitch."

Will flicked the switch for the overhead light. It was burned out. He reached over—slow, real slow—to flip on the headlights again. All his resting muscles came awake and hurt him. He knew he'd been sitting there tight as a fiddle string and not resting at all.

"I got to have some goddamn light. I'm no animal. I can't see in the dark like you seem to do."

Marco had his head back, eyes closed, suffering.

"Jesus, you bastard, don't tell me you're asleep." Somehow the idea seemed to frighten Will.

Marco opened his eyes as though he'd heard. He looked at the twin cones of light boring holes through the rainy night. With some show of pain, he moved his damaged arm forward to the glove compartment and thumbed it open.

The cab lurched no more than an inch. It seemed a fall of a mile that would never end, to those trapped in the truck.

Marco pulled out a repair lamp, its protective wire cage around the bulb and its extension cord all coiled neatly around itself.

The other end of the cord had a gadget that fitted into the cigarette lighter and ran off the truck's battery. He handed it to Will with a gesture that indicated Will could plug it in without disturbing the truck's precarious balance.

Marco snapped his fingers to attract Will's attention. Will looked up from the glowing bulb in his hands and caught the direction of the deaf-mute's glance. Nodding that he understood, Will shut off the headlamps to conserve the battery.

The lamp was a comfort. And a curse. A curse because now Will could see Marco's eyes. They were regarding him softly. Were they asking Will Carney to make the necessary moves to save them all? Or did they say that since it was his, Marco's, fault that they all were in this deadly place, that he was sorry. Or did those eyes, which seemed to bore through him, reflect the hatred that Will deserved, the contempt he often saw in the eyes of his charges?

Will had to turn away from the blood-spattered figure beside him. He stared out the front window, out into the certain death that awaited them all.

There was no comfort there either.

It was early morning when the carnival hit the crossroad collection of shacks, general store, café, and gas station—a small place without even a name to be remembered.

The entire troupe was bone-weary from traveling all night and the emptiness in their bellies. Paulette complained the most.

She'll be complaining one hell of a lot more, Will thought, when I tell her there's no money for breakfast and she'll have to eat out of cans for her meal. The few bucks they'd scraped up in the last town of any size had gone for gas and oil. Not all of it. The rest had gone into the pocket of a gambler in a roadside tavern. The gambler had smiled wider and his hands had moved faster than Will's.

Of course, they both had been cheating and everybody knew it, but the gambler had been a much better cheater. Will might have got some of it back as he had done in the past, except that Marco was off asleep somewhere and the town sharpie had a lot of his heavyset, red-necked friends hanging around.

So now it was "Dead Broke in a Morning Crossroads and Hope for a Penny."

As soon as the truck pulled to a stop, Paulette hurried off as fast as she could waddle to relieve herself. Serena, the Moon Child, followed more slowly.

Marco went off to look for any heavy, manual-labor

chores that could buy a loaf of bread and top off the gas tank. Colonel John, the Midget, went along with the Strong Man to speak for him.

Will and Pepino, the Rubber Man, went into the café. The screen door, which was holed through and kept out only the most stupid of flies, slammed shut behind them.

Christ, Will thought, I'd never ask for another thing if I just never had to hear another goddamn screen door slam shut on another empty morning.

They each took a seat on the cracked leatherette stools and Will reached over for a well-stained menu. He fingered it in a thoughtful way.

"What'll it be?" the counterman asked without enthusiasm.

"Can I tell you the truth?" Will said, and he smiled the way he did when he wanted something.

The counterman swatted a fly, smashing it on the greasy counter top. He scraped the bloody mess off the surface of the counter with the edge of the flyswatter.

Will looked up from the menu, the beguiling smile still in place. "Can I tell you the truth?"

"I already know it," the counterman finally admitted, chewing on a bedraggled toothpick.

Will frowned. "Well, then, that is perfectly marvelous. Maybe I could ask you to join up with us." It was not a serious offer.

"Nah. I get a full belly right where I am. Not like some folks."

The man looked at Will with little pig eyes, waiting for the inevitable story, waiting but not particularly interested. He'd heard them all anyway, every con in the book.

Will touched Pepino on his back. "You ever see anything the like of this? Show him a little something, Pepino."

The Rubber Man seemed to melt where he sat, arms

becoming liquid, his limbs curling in the most extraordinary way, setting the stool spinning beneath him.

"Tell him not to break the goddamn seat," the counterman said.

"Now what's that worth?" Will asked.

"Not a goddamn thing."

"Show him another trick, Pepino." Will's smile was wearing a trifle thin.

"Shove your tricks. They won't buy you nothing here," said the counterman, folding his arms across his chest.

The man looked up at the banging sound of the screen door and his mouth fell open about halfway to his belly button.

"Godamighty!" He was staring at Paulette in the doorway. It was a double door. Even so, she was making it an effort to squeeze through. "Jesus H. Particular Christ! I thought my Aunt Hattie was fat but I never seen the like of that one."

Paulette made it through the door and moved over to the soft-drink case. It was the only thing in the room big enough for her to sit down on.

Will tugged at his chin thoughtfully. Almost shyly he said, "Now what's that worth to you."

The man, however, wasn't listening. He was staring with no lessening wonder at Serena. She stood in the doorway, framed there in the morning light, looking like something that had escaped from the land of dwarves, trolls, and fairies.

"She looks like a big . . . like a big, white rabbit!" breathed the man. The flyswatter dropped from his hand.

He glanced back to Paulette who, with incredible nimbleness for one her size, hoisted herself up on the soft-drink case and smiled ecstatically, as though she could feel the coolness beneath her through her bloomers.

"Are you over by the gentleman who is talking, Will?"

Serena said in her honeyed voice. It was not really a question. She already knew.

"I'm here, darling. Come along. There's nothing in between."

Serena walked hesitantly across the floor, unafraid but careful.

"Godamighty!" the man said again.

It wasn't bad enough that Serena had been born an albino, with no pigment in her skin and hair. Not curse enough to be born with moon-pale eyes and gone blind to boot. The real horror was that nature had given her a beautiful face. It had given her a long, graceful neck, like a column of shimmering talc, and gave her a pair of breasts like white downy peaches and arms that were so graceful—along with the perfectly formed hands at the ends of them it—made you want to weep. Because that's where it all stopped. From the hips down, her legs were stunted, misshapen, and thin as rails. The little baby shoes she wore on her feet made it all seem the more horrible, somehow.

"Now, what's that worth to you, you cold-hearted son of a bitch?" Will said in the softest of voices, so that the man couldn't really hear it all. He said it in a way that blamed the man for Serena and what she was.

Serena came over to the counter and sat down gracefully upon a stool. The counterman stared at her some more and then looked at Will. The counterman hadn't been born yesterday. His eyes grew hard as marbles.

"You got some money to pay for breakfast? No? Then get the hell out of my place," said the man, returning to himself and to what he was.

"Oh, it's yours, is it. Mighty lucky man. Pretty well set up, you are. Other people," said Will pointedly, "are not so lucky. See here, I'll make you a bargain."

"Both parties have to have something to make a bargain."

Will handed Serena the menu.

"This poor girl can't see. She's blind as a stone. You don't believe it? Test her any way you want to. Light a match and poke it in her eye. Go on. Go on," urged Will.

The man shook his head.

"Then if you believe me, I'm going to show you a most wondrous thing. You think this poor creature's been put upon by the Lord? Well, she has, that's clear enough. But He gave her a gift for the mistake He made in the fashion of her. The tips of her beautiful fingers."

The man looked down at Serena's hands and beautiful they were.

"The tips of her beautiful fingers are so sensitive that she can read print with them. Not raised print like they make for the blind. No sir, not those little dots. No sir. Common old print of the page. Newspaper, book, or this menu she holds in her hand. Now the bargain's this," and here Will came alive with new energy, for this was what he was all about. "If she can read the menu with only the tips of her beautiful fingers, will you stand six poor wayfarers to a decent meal?"

"Six? Six of you?" echoed the man stupidly.

Colonel John the Midget walked in with Marco the Strong Man. There was a frown on his face.

"Nobody out back in the garage," said the Midget.

"That's all right, Colonel John," Will said. "This lucky man here owns the whole kit and kaboodle, I'll just bet."

The counterman was looking at the Midget now, though the Colonel was far less a wonder, almost a commonplace, after what he had seen so far.

"Will you do it, friend?" said Will, his voice like honey as it poured from his tongue. "And besides, we'll do what chores we can around here until noon. Paulette and Serena do marvelous needlework. Marco—the Strong Man there—and me can do some heavy cleaning up, and the Colonel, small as he is, can lend a hand. What say, friend, would you see this wonder or no?"

The man nodded dumbly. "Have her read it."

Serena ran her fingers over the menu, hesitating here and there over a grease stain or a bit of dried mustard. Then, in a clear, sweet voice, she read off without mistakes the man's refreshment list to him.

The counterman nodded again, like a stupid puppet with a broken head string. His eyes were wide with uncomprehending wonder.

"All right then, I'll feed you, but first I got to get the kids up to see this. Hell, it's like having our own damned private circus."

He pulled his apron off and disappeared through the swinging door alongside the grill, and they could hear him rousing his young ones in an excited, festive voice.

Will Carney smiled all around to let his charges know that he'd taken care of them once again.

The truck shuddered as some loose rock peppered it from above and Will like to wet himself.

"Save us, damn it! Save us!" He half laughed because he thought he heard someone ask "Why?" Now that was a question wasn't it? "Why?"

"In the name of the Juggler," he whispered to himself.

The counterman had come back and started slapping bacon and eggs on the griddle. He kept glancing wondering glances back at one and all. Now that he was paying for them, he wanted to enjoy all of the sight of them that he could.

Then the swinging door opened and three sleepy girls, dressed in the shifts they slept in, came stumbling into the café. Did they pull up short! They were dumbfounded and opened their mouths just like their daddy did, the better perhaps to catch unwary flies.

Will's own mouth dropped an inch before he laid on his best grin.

One of the brute's daughters, late in her teens, was as pretty as sin and just as willing. She caught Will's secret grin, meant only for her, and the wanting behind it. She batted her eyes and flicked her little tongue out to wet her lips suggestively.

She smiled back in such a way that Will knew he had only to figure the place and the privacy. Oh yes, how good days did sometimes follow bad.

And deadly nights, peaceful ones as well.

Serena the blind albino lived a secret life inside herself. Inside, in that strange and fragile dream house that was her mind, she was a being of great and seldom-used power. This great power came to her unasked, caught her quite by surprise. At first, it was only a dream. But, like all dreams, it contained the idea of death.

It was a power that never came to her in any other fashion than as a dream, yet it grew, taking on a life—almost a reality—of its own.

And it was a powerful dream, a gentle dream, an understanding dream, and, sometimes when she willed it, a fatal one. Yes. Fatal. For with it, this gentlest of all gentle creatures had killed and would kill again, that was a certainty. For what was power if it was not meant to be used.

Blind, loving Serena made a strange executioner.

The first death she dreamed into being was more an act of kindness than murder, even if it was her own father.

Serena was born in Baltimore, Maryland, once called the City of White Steps because it had been the special pride of the good housewives in the old town to sweep and scrub with soap and brush the stone porches, sidewalks, and even the cobblestone streets. She was raised in one of the better neighborhoods.

Lace curtains enhanced the tall windows of the row houses built in another and better age. Each house had trees—carefully ringed with white-painted, wrought-iron cages—planted opposite the front door. The doors themselves were freshly painted each year and were rich with shining brass. The houses were many-roomed, elegantly appointed, and clustered together in an architectural ring of beauty—a haven for the well-to-do—beseiged, surrounded on all sides by zones of vice and human misery.

The black ghetto engulfed this fading world of yesterday's elegance. Not all at once, but gradually, with each passing year. Indirectly, this slow transition abetted the death of Serena's father.

With the passage of time, the cobblestones were tarred over to make better surfaces for the automobile. The horses and carriages that had once thundered down the streets were gone. With the coming of war upon war, the wrought-iron cages and gates were torn up in patriotic zeal and offered for scrap.

The world changed, got older and tired and the white stone of old Baltimore grew grey and the sidewalks fell into disrepair. Once-gracious houses were broken up into tenements, all the grace and majesty of what had gone before disappeared under the grinding hell of poverty, under the terrible reality of life in the black ghetto.

In the very heart of this ghetto, there stood a strong anachronism, a single house which withstood the ravages wrought by the jungle of the city. In this house, which would soon know murder, the world outside seldom entered. It's windows were still veiled with delicate lace curtains in a pattern of bluebirds holding cartouches of ribbons in their beaks. The boot scraper at the door was painted shining black and the stone steps were freshly painted white every three months. Even the shadows cast by the surviving trees opposite the front door—and still caged in wrought iron—seemed undimmed by the dirt and filth of the overindustrialized city. The trees budded in spring with the very palest of green.

The children of the ghetto—for no reason they could or would explain—respected the caged trees and the house and the people who lived within it. They were—the people who lived in this strange house—in their fashion, the neighborhood's private mystery and special treasure.

The people who lived within the mystery were white gentry whose bloodlines went so far back in the history of the pre-Civil War South that they seemed wrapped in magnolia and legend.

The husband, Enoch Pratt, was frequently consulted by various historical societies, for he was the possessor of a most unique library of long-out-of-print books concerning Baltimore's history. He had made of himself the curator of the past. A curiosity lay in the fact that he was unaware of it. He saw himself, did Enoch Pratt, as very much a keeper of the present. It was not his fault that his present was everyone else's past.

Enoch dressed in slender trousers with elastic straps that looped beneath the insteps of his short boots, a style fifty years out of date. His shirts were made by an old firm that kept the pattern in use in order to fill the occasional requests of theatrical costumers and historical-drama societies. The sleeves were puffed at the wrists, the front heavy with pleating, and the collars high.

His wife, Mary, also dressed in the fashion of the 1800s, her hair always in the intricate, curled fashion of days gone by.

Their dealings with the outside world were conducted almost exclusively through tradesmen who delivered. They subscribed to no newspapers or magazines, had no radio, and generally lived as if what was so was not so.

It was a rare and exceedingly fine madness.

Of course, in avoiding the world so completely, it changed all around them and they were unaware of it. What they believed to be so became so, as far as they were concerned.

Their principal outing of the year occurred upon the seventh of October. Upon that day, they traveled— largely afoot, since their attempts to hire a horse-drawn carriage presented great difficulty—to Westminster Churchyard.

There they placed a rose-encrusted wreath upon the grave of Edgar Allan Poe.

They almost never spoke to the people they passed on the street. Upon occasion they would nod to the verger of Westminster Church and he would nod in return and wish a good day to Mr. and Mrs. Enoch Pratt.

Enoch would regale his wife on their return journey— back to their home and to the century that was more to their liking—with the oft-told tale of how it had been his own great-great-great-grandfather who had long ago published many of Edgar Allan Poe's works.

It was from that same publishing house—printers of textbooks and inspirational works—that the Pratts derived their income, that stipend that allowed them to deny nearly all that had happened in the world since the death of Poe.

They were both quite mad but not dangerously so.

In the year 1940, a natural thing happened that they could not deny. Mary Pratt became pregnant. She took to her bed and eventually delivered a baby girl in the same bed it had been conceived in.

The family doctor, an old man who loved them in their gentle madness, took Enoch aside and explained a bit more of the facts of heredity than Enoch, till then, had been aware of. Their child had been born afflicted with albinoism.

"And this albinoism, pray tell, what is its cause?" Enoch Pratt asked.

"It may be from a total absence of pigmentation cells, interference with their migration to their intended locations during development of the embryo, or the lack of the necessary hormonal stimulation."

"Ah," said Enos, no more enlightened than before. "And what is the reason for its appearance?"

The doctor hesitated, on the edge of knowledge he was reluctant to reveal. "Consanguinity can figure into it prominently."

Enoch smiled rather coldly. "I see. At least, I think I do. Then you are saying it is a punishment for marrying first cousin to first cousin?"

"Not a punishment but a consequence, perhaps," the doctor said, unruffled in the face of Enoch's own illusion. The doctor had known them both since they were children. The truth was, Mary was Enoch's own sister, not his first cousin. Perhaps it was incest, and their pretence that what had happened did not happen, that had driven the Pratts into full retreat into another century. In any case, it was not the doctor's concern; it was the child who had to be dealt with.

"What special care must be given to the child?"

"She lacks the pigmentation that normally screens against light rays. The sun will be a great danger to her," cautioned the doctor.

A small smile that might be described as complacent, or even self-satisfied, quirked the corners of Enoch's mouth.

"Even her eyes lack protection. They will be painfully sensitive to light."

Enoch's smile broadened.

"Well, then, what a perfect place for her to have been born. We rarely leave the house and the shades are nearly always drawn," he said with rather perfect logic.

The doctor sighed, placed his hands on his knees, and stood up. Perhaps Enoch was right. What better place for a moon child to be born than into a fairy tale?

When the little one first opened her eyes in the soft glow of candlelight, they were not much dazzled. They did, however, sparkle with those red reflections that mark the gaze of the albino. The irises were the palest of gray and somewhat wispy, like the rings that often surround the autumn moon.

"Oh, what a love! What a delight!" Enoch cooed, as his wife smiled softly in the near-dark with equal delight.

And in their own little world, it all seemed right and proper.

In time, the fairy tale acquired dark moments of its own. It was discovered that Serena—for that was the name they chose for her—had incapacities much greater than a simple loss of pigmentation. The doctor came to examine her and diagnosed that she suffered, as well, from a congenital atrophy of the lower limbs. Serena's natural functions would not be impaired—through therapy she would walk after a fashion—but gone would be the running, jumping, leaping joys of normal childhood.

The doctor's heart ached when he had to offer news of this new disaster to Enoch, but Enoch only smiled again.

"It is a pity, of course, but, then, what better household could a child who will suffer difficulty in getting about be born into? We have no need of the world outside of this house."

The doctor nodded as he put his instruments back into his battered black bag. As he prepared to take his leave of them, he pondered the fact that God, apparently, had prepared the child for the best life it could hope for in this strange home.

Serena was given a room of her own when she was six. It was adorned with murals illuminating the stories of the Grimms and Hans Christian Andersen. The colors were so pale as to be the merest breath of color. Still, as a backdrop to the luminous child, they were crashingly vivid. The room was filled with the plush toys of a bygone era. White rabbits, white elephants, white mice, and white ducks with pale yellow bills. There were shelves filled with old-fashioned picture books of another age.

Enoch commissioned a young artist and a young writer to create a small book telling the tale of "Serena, Moon Child" in a gentle, loving, and fantastic way. One copy only was printed which made it, by far, the most expensive of all children's books. Further adventures appeared every year until she was twelve. It was in that year that she began to go blind.

For the first and only time, Enoch cried over the trials of his little fairy princess and wondered about the wisdom of his marriage. Mary took the news with greater courage. Serena took it with the greatest courage of all. She asked that a chair, with pillows piled high, be placed in the front window so that she could see and store up visions of the world.

The black children of the neighborhood wondered about the magic child and were always silent when they passed by her window. They would wave and smile at her and she would wave and smile in return. Sometimes, they brought small gifts, deposited furtively on the doorstep. A ball, a rag doll, a small bag of marbles. They were, in a way, offerings to a goddess.

Sometimes the children stood on the sidewalk and whispered their whispers to her, even though from that distance it would have been impossible for her to hear them. Somehow, they believed, she would mysteriously know, and in some magical way, make their wishes come true.

It took a full year before her sight was completely gone.

Serena feared the velvet dark at first and regretted desperately that she could no longer read. She did, for a time, become hypersensitive to the touch of anything upon her. The doctor feared a new affliction. It passed away in time, though a great sensitivity of touch stayed in her hands.

Not long after she went totally blind, Serena discovered, quite by chance, that she could read the slight impressions left by type upon the page in the normal way of printing. Knowing the shapes of letters, she was able to read the large typefaces, and then smaller ones, until her hands would fly across the pages like tiny, white hummingbirds. Her hands moved so quickly, interpreting the slightly engraved surface, that she saw nearly as well as someone with the gift of sight.

There was a second gift that awaited her, that did not awaken until it was needed—a more awesome, almost terrible gift.

Serena's blindness was a blow that shattered Enoch Pratt's entire fabric of fantasy. His marriage, his whole fantastic retreat from the world, came crashing down around his ears. The world around him suddenly became evil, cold, and unforgiving.

His marriage had taken on the evil aspects of the doomed in the tales of his beloved Edgar Allan Poe.

Enoch saw himself somehow trapped in a tale more macabre than any his idol, Poe, had ever created. In his despair, he took to drink.

And passed eventually into a madness deeper and more terrifying than any Poe had ever dreamed of. Awake or asleep, he lived in a phantasm, a living hell eating at the edges of his being. He became aware—suddenly, it seemed—that his white family, his milk-white girl, were living in a sea of black faces. One night, drunk, he left the house and walked through the neighborhood, hair disheveled and eyes wild.

He stumbled down the mean streets, his mind aflame with tormented images, made all the more hideous in the garish neon-lit streets of the century he had too long denied.

Serena's second gift awoke in her. It was in the shape of a dream. She lay on a coverlet of light silk and dreamed. Her father's madness, his pain filled the dream.

Enoch moved among the blacks, screaming, "Get back to the plantation!"

Hostile eyes impaled him, conversations halted, and a silent storm of faces turned to consider this strange apparition from the past walking before them.

The madness was upon him full tilt. The old hates and prejudices of another century swam in his brain like blind cave fish. Enoch waved his arms at them, screaming, "Don't you darkies know your masters will take good care of you? Don't do this foolish thing! Where will you go? What will you do?"

A black child tried to take his hand and lead him back home. She did not understand this strangely dressed white man's rage or his madness. She only knew he belonged, somehow, to the magic child in the house, and she thought he might be lost.

Enoch, with misguided zeal, stooped down and tried to embrace the little girl.

"Ginny Mae, you come here! Ginny Mae!" the little girl's older sister yelled from the stoop of an old house. "You stay away from that crazy white man!"

"He's okay. It's only Mr. Pratt," said Ginny Mae.

The sister came down off the stoop and swept the little girl aside, putting herself between the white man and the child.

Enoch cried out and stumbled toward the black girl, his arms outstretched to take her to his breast.

"Lord," he cried. "Don't talk like that to your master, Mandy. I'll save you!"

The girl slapped out at him as his hands touched her. She shoved him back, more embarrassed than frightened. "Get away from me. Crazy-ass Honky!" she screamed at him, figuring if the shove didn't keep him away the shout would.

A well-dressed black man, sitting in his flashy Cadillac, a stranger to this neighborhood, slammed his car door open and strode out into the street. Say, who that bastard think he is, anyway?

"Hey! Hey! What you doing, you white bastard? Raping this sweet girl, now?" said the well-dressed black dude.

Enoch whirled around to face the deep voice, the threat at his back. "I will save her from the mistake of freedom!" he cried. "She'll go home or know the taste of the overseer's whip!"

The dude punched him in the mouth, busting out Enoch's front teeth, smashing him to the pavement. He hadn't meant to hit him so hard. It was that edge of madness in Enoch's voice that had thrown him, scared him even, made him swing so hard at what frightened him.

Serena jerked in her sleep. Enoch's madness whirled through her own mind, the pain and rage and terrible loss. Mixed in with these things was something deeper, a drive more demanding. Guilt. Shame. Enoch had sinned, sinned in a way only death could cleanse. I must die. I must be punished. I want to die. Yes, those were the innermost thoughts tumbling in his mad brain.

These thoughts were as clear in Serena's dream as if they were printed on a page for her fingers to read.

"Good Christ, stop that, mister," the girl yelled at the top of her voice, angry because things were getting out of hand. "You had no call to hit him like that."

Her little sister hid her face in her skirt, hiding the sight of bloodied Enoch on the ground.

"Man trying to rape you or something," said the black man defensively.

The older sister said, with some heat, "You get along now. He ain't trying to rape nobody!"

Rape?

The word seemed to act as a magnet. The word went flying around the crowd on the street, triggering hard feelings. The blacks gathered, sensitive to the word and the meaning.

There was blood all over Enoch's face and his ruffled shirt. His ruined mouth opened and closed spasmodically. The girl stepped between the fallen man and the man from the Cadillac who had knocked him down.

She roughly shouldered the man aside. "You quit, now. I know this man. He done suffered enough. Didn't have no harm in him. He just a little weird in the head, is all. He been hurt enough. You leave him be."

The black man still had his fists clenched. The faces in the crowd all around were still hostile.

The older sister bent down and helped Enoch to his feet. He seemed dazed, the shock of the blow rendering him senseless. He staggered, almost fell. His eyes saw, not this world but into another—Poe's dead world—and it was his own grave his wild eyes sought.

The black girl's hand on his arm steadied him. This act of helping him to his feet eased the tension in the watching crowd. The anger began to recede like a storm with spent force.

But this was not as Enoch wished it.

Serena in her dream, saw it all. Her father, that poor, mad, frightened creature, with pains and hates too large for this world. This man, so unlike her father, with a horrifying need that only death could cure, stood before her, as if begging her for mercy, for that release from this life he so desperately wanted.

Serena then understood it was more than a dream. The dream grew, pulsing with energy and sudden force, until it became a torrent in her head, a giddy rush to power, awesome, limitless power. She saw the grave Enoch so desperately sought, the violent punishment his mind and body shrieked to have.

And to that end, she moved what did not have the strength to move.

Serena nearly screamed in her sleep, a smile of secret knowledge on her delicate lips. She went back inside her brain, deep into the hidden places, until, in that secret, terrible place, she at last understood what she must do. There had to be an end to Enoch's shame, to a lifetime of hurt, and anguish that would not stop.

It was like sticking a knife into a living creature, but she did it. She reached into a wish in Enoch's mind and made death love him.

Enoch's eyes glazed, his unsteady legs stiffened with a surge of adrenaline. His face was suffused with his own madness. His hands clenched and unclenched, now fists, now like the claws of some great, predatory bird.

The people in the hostile crowd were beginning to move off, their anger vented, the crisis over.

His eyes focused and he looked all about him, a quick, all-inclusive glance, and saw for the first time, a world he had pretended against all his life. He saw the ugliness of the city ghetto, the squalid, sordid hustle of the age in which he really lived. With this sudden clarity of mind, came, unbidden, an act—unthinkable, unspeakable— against everything Enoch had ever known or thought.

His hands went up, reaching for the girl. It happened very quickly. His fingers found the neck of her thin cotton dress and, adrenaline strong, he ripped it down to her waist, exposing her white bra.

The crowd fell on him like lions. Had they not seen some crazy white man laying hands on one of their sisters? They stamped him into the pavement. Yes, yes, Enoch's mind cried, my just punishment. The weight of the angry crowd, hard shoes and fists, raining down on him, turned him from a human being into a bloodied pulp. They killed him, there in the street, pounding him into an almost unrecognizable lump of human meat, just two blocks away from the house with the lace curtains and the gentle moon-child dreaming his death in the window.

It was, in Serena's heart, in Enoch's mind, an act of kindness.

Enoch was gone but, somehow, nothing much seemed changed. There were all sorts of things to take care of, people to see, arrangements to make, deliveries to be made, checks filled out, that sort of thing. Mary Pratt was frail, however, and so a nurse was brought in—at first, to help in the taking care of Serena, and, later, taking care of Mary, who took to her bed soon after her husband's death, obsessed with the idea that she was pregnant again with Serena, her first born.

The power that gentle Serena invoked, subsided. Like the dream from which it sprang, it returned into that deep and secret place in her mind, to await another time and place suitable for its invoking.

Serena felt no guilt, no great remorse. She mourned Enoch's death in the spirit of one who has lost someone beloved, but her grief was tempered by a feeling of justice rendered, of mercy tendered.

Her father could not love life as it was.

So she had made death love him, where life could not.

In her own way, too, Serena understood her mother's madness.

It was a madness without pain. She saw it very clearly on the days she sat in her window, carefully sifting through the world about her in dreams.

Mary Pratt's madness was a joyful one, the expectant mother of an imaginary fetus.

Serena sensed no need for death, no great longing for it as her father had experienced. And so Serena's dreams were more like caresses than inquiries, as she sometimes probed the gentle madness in her mother.

Serena often sat beside her mother's bed for long hours, listening to her talk of the child yet to come.

"I shall call her Serena. It will be a girl, I am sure. A woman knows these things," said Mary Pratt, touching her empty belly, trying to sense the unmistakable stirrings of new life inside her. "Did you feel that? She kicked me! I felt it." Mary's face was rapturous.

"Yes, Mother." Serena stroked her face. They spent many long hours in just this way.

Sometimes Serena read fairy stories to her mother from a big, colored book that only her fingers could see. Mary Pratt listened with obvious delight, thinking to herself that some day she would read those very same stories to her child when it came.

Serena was twenty-two when Will Carney came calling. He'd gone to buy an ice-cream suit and some frilled-front shirts from the very same tailor to whom Enoch Pratt had once given his custom.

The salesman was something of a gossip and something of a historian of the bizarre. He had too little to think about and too much to say. The tailor mentioned Enoch Pratt, who had lived, almost, in another century. He talked about the strange house with drawn curtains. He spoke of the enigmatic, reclusive moon child, Serena. While he talked, the tailor glanced often at Will's crippled, scar-laced hand as though suggesting that Will, himself maimed in some small way, might appreciate a story of someone really put upon by fate.

"You say her hair is pure white?" Will Carney asked, his mind spinning with the notion.

"Like a winter full of snow, like milkweed. Didn't I just say it? I've seen her myself, sitting in the window of their house on Rain Street," said the tailor.

"And her eyes are pink?"

"They seem so when the sun strikes them."

"Can't walk? Just sits in that chair all day?"

"Oh, she can walk. But her legs are like toothpicks and about as long. How she's able to walk on them at all is a miracle in itself."

Will Carney thought about this, becoming more and more intrigued.

"But the rest of it—her being blind, yet able to read regular print with the tips of her fingers—is just so much gossip?" asked Will, his eyes bright as new copper coins.

"No. It's God's truth. So I been told by people have actually seen her about it, and, mind you, there'd be no cause for them to lie. It's an ungodly thing and not well thought of by some I could mention." The salesman bent forward over the counter and said in a confidential tone, "Of course, there's folks always against something they can't figure out. I've heard some mighty strange things about the Pratts. Unnatural things. Wicked things."

"No doubt," said Will Carney.

"I'm not one to tell tales," said the tailor, preparing to do just that.

"Save it," said Will, who had heard enough and more.

Will bought a polka-dot tie to go with his off-the-rack

suit and frilled-front shirt. He bought a straw skimmer as well, hanging it on his head at a rakish angle.

Will went to Rain Street and found the house. He just had to see that wonder he'd been told about and there she was, sitting in the window as advertised. Good God, but she was beautiful. The tailor hadn't mentioned that. She was goddamned, unbelievably beautiful. It was a face like no other he had ever seen.

He just stood there and marveled over the sight for a long time. Serena smiled, deep in her dreams. Will looked on in unrestrained wonder. To find such a thing as this, this delicate snow-white creature in the window, was something for which Will had longed for all his life.

There had to be some way to possess this wonder, to use it for his own ends.

He turned it over in his mind for a long time.

When Will Carney came calling, he'd found out all he could about Enoch Pratt and his madness. He found out about the yearly visits to the grave of Edgar Allan Poe. He even went so far as to read the books Poe had written, although it had given him somewhat of a headache and left him as much at a loss as when he started reading them. Still, he wanted something to talk about to get him inside that house, and it was the best thing that came to mind.

He rang the antique doorknocker and after quite some

time, the nurse opened the door. The nurse frowned at his cheerful way of saying hello.

Will asked to see Mr. Enoch Pratt.

"Been dead for years," the woman said and started to close the heavy oaken door.

"See here," said Will. "I'm that shocked!"

The woman refrained from closing the door, staring at Will warily, wondering what he was about. In truth, she did not like the slick look of him.

Will Carney frowned and pursed his lips. (He'd been told he was no mean actor.) He removed his hat and scratched his head with his bad hand.

"It's a marvel I never heard about it. Of course, I've been in Europe on my studies and that great man may well have passed on while I was gone."

"Great man?" the woman echoed in doubt and suspicion. She had heard him described as crazy often enough, but a great man?

"For certain, madam. He was a great scholar of that greatest of all Southern—perhaps of all American—writers, Edgar Allan Poe."

"I wouldn't know about that."

Undaunted, Will went on. "Why, his collection of Poe memorabilia is world famous. His collection concerning the history of Baltimore is no small shuck, either. Now, Mrs. Pratt, I wonder if . . ."

"I am not Mrs. Pratt. I'm her nurse and companion."

Will frowned. This was more difficult than he'd imagined.

There was a piping sound from inside the room to the right of the door. It had the clarity of a bell.

"Who is it? Who's there, Agnes?" the voice asked.

"I don't know, Miss Serena," said the nurse, with the thought in her mind that she didn't want to know.

"Well, whoever it is, tell him to come into the parlor," said the voice, ever so sweetly.

"I don't think so, Miss Serena," said the nurse, taking in Will Carney head to toe with one disparaging glance.

"I do, Agnes. I really do think you should show the gentleman into the parlor."

The nurse frowned, but could really see no harm in it as long as she was there to see nothing underhanded was attempted. Whatever this man was selling, he would make his pitch, fail in that, and soon be gone. What harm could there be in that?

And Serena, that poor, lonely creature, had no friends, no other voice but her own, her mad mother's, the kindly doctor who ministered to their needs, and an occasional tradesman. Another voice, no matter how absurd a thing it proposed, might be good for Serena. It might entertain her for a little while, anyway. With that thought, Agnes ushered Will in.

Will Carney held his hat in his hands and bowed to Serena stiffly from the waist when Serena insisted on the nurse introducing them. Serena smiled at Will and there was enchantment in it. She ordered tea for both of them.

Will took the chair opposite Serena when it was offered. The sight of her legs thrust straight out upon the flowered cushions gave him a start. If she had heard or sensed it, she gave no sign. She poured the tea herself and reached out her hands to serve him. When he took the cup and saucer from her, his hand brushed against hers.

"I am sorry," she said.

"Sorry, yes, for what?"

"For the injury to your hand."

"You could tell that just by brushing your hand against mine by accident?"

"Yes."

"That is a wonder."

Will came every day at about the same hour and they sat
and chatted together. One day, he met Mary, the mother,
who smiled at him vaguely and simpered prettily at his
flattering compliments. All the while, he was scheming
how to make profit out of all of this. By the end of the
week, the nurse trusted him enough to leave Will and
Serena alone.

The doctor, during his regular visits, was pleased at the
animation that seemed to spark Serena because of Will's
visits. However, the doctor wondered secretly if the poor,
afflicted child was falling in love.

When they were left alone, Will Carney spoke to Serena
of the wonders of the great, wide world and made her
hunger for it. She revealed her magical ability to read the
printed page with her fingers. Oh, what an attraction she
was going to be if he could manage it.

There was only one thing for it.

"I've come to love your daughter, Mrs. Pratt."

He looked first at Mary Pratt and then to Serena. The
moon girl's face shone with the love of being loved. In that
moment, Will said to himself that he wouldn't ever ask for
another thing if only that beautiful creature could be
made whole and perfect. Not to get her sight back—that
was perhaps asking too much of Providence—but only to
have her legs grow as pretty as the rest of her.

"I want to make her my wife."

Mary Pratt clapped her hands for the romance of it. That she should find it objectionable did not occur to her. However, the nurse-companion called the doctor at once.

He came running. He looked Will Carney over with a sharp eye and didn't like what he saw now that Will wanted to be more than a casual visitor of an afternoon. The doctor checked into Will's past and found out what Will was. Will hadn't been particularly careful about hiding his past. He had left too many clues and loose ends, too many mistakes with his name on them.

The doctor told Mary and he told Serena. Mary cried because it addled her head to have to decide about things like what was right or wrong, good or bad.

But Serena only nodded her head and smiled.

"He's a liar and a cheat. A charlatan. A carnival man. He's unstable and shiftless. He's had a sordid past and will have undoubtably a rotten future, if he has any at all. He is trouble. Born to it and bound to inflict it on Serena. He is all that and more. I've heard certain stories, stories I am too genteel to repeat. Suffice it to say, the man is an out-and-out scoundrel." The doctor's face was red with barely suppressed fury.

"I know," Serena said. And she did know. After all, hadn't she gone back inside herself often enough, back into that special dream-place that told her all she needed to know of this man Will Carney and more besides? Perhaps she and she alone understood who this man was, saw the true face hidden beneath Will Carney's façade.

"You know?" said the doctor, with disbelief. "But how could you? You've no experience with the real world, with this kind of man."

"I could read it in his face when I touched him," she said, and it was true, for she could see people in more than one way.

"Then you can see it's out of the question. I can't allow it."

"On the contrary, you can't stop it, doctor," said Serena.

"I can. I will. I'm trustee of your father's estate. I'll go to law to see that this jackanapes doesn't marry the heiress he thinks you to be."

"I'm of legal age," Serena said with determination.

"I'll do everything in my power to stop it," said the doctor stubbornly.

Serena just shook her head. "You don't understand. Not truly, nor can I make you understand. Be happy for me. I am quite happy for myself." She reached out and covered the doctor's rough hand with her small, delicately boned fingers. "Besides, you don't have power over me or my life. I let you think it so because it gives you comfort."

"But Serena . . ." the old man began, the shadow of tears in the corners of his eyes.

"Be still, my old and beloved friend. I don't need to be protected from the world. It has been so but I never wished it. I've been sitting in the window all the afternoons of my life waiting for the one, waiting for a Will Carney to come and take me out into the world."

But the doctor was not swayed.

He offered Will Carney three thousand dollars for Will to leave and never come back. Will pretended shock and injury to his heart.

"You're afraid I want the money that might come to her from her father's publishing business. I don't. I'll tell you that."

"Will you sign a paper to that effect?" said the doctor quickly, sure he had Will backed into a corner with that one.

But Will surprised him.

Will smiled and said, "I'll sign anything you damn well please."

The doctor had a paper drawn up and put him to the test. Will signed it without hesitation but the old doctor wasn't in the least bit satisfied. What, however, could he do? He sensed there was much pain and trouble for Serena in this flashy young man, who could lie as easy by smile or word of mouth as others could breathe.

Still, what else but pain and terrible loneliness did Serena have inside this strange house? Could he in all consciousness, prevent her from trying her wings, from flying, even if she was only to crash to the ground a stone's throw away?

"But it can't be love. It isn't that. You want to make a public show of her! Isn't that your plan, sir?" the doctor accused Will.

Will took it in stride. "I am a man of the carnival. It's the way I make my bread and no shame in it. I've got a fat lady, a midget, a rubber man and a mute strong man in my company. It might look like small shakes to you but I don't mean to stay that way. I've got my ambitions. I've got my dreams."

"My point. Just my point," insisted the doctor. "Your only aim is to exploit Serena's . . . her condition."

Will Carney stared across the table at the man who stood between him and his dream.

"Hell! What kind of life has she got now? I want to give her a life outside this mausoleum she's trapped in."

"The humiliation will kill her."

Will was angered by that, almost more than he intended to be. "Humiliation! Humiliation to know that she can earn her own bread, make her own way in the world, have people around her to talk to. You yourself know its what she needs to get her through the long lonely days, else what was the purpose in letting me come around if not to bring some color and life and excitement into her life?"

"You presume to . . ."

But Will hadn't finished. "Damn, you insult me, sir, and my friends. We may not be your kind of people, Doctor, but we are people just the same. If these were other days, I'd have to ask you to step outside and settle this."

"If I were twenty years younger I'd . . ." began the doctor, clenching his fists and then stopping, letting it pass. There seemed no getting around it.

In the end, a compromise was reached. Serena would go with Will Carney but there would be no marriage. It was better than Will had hoped for. There had been a terrible sickness in him when he thought of getting into the conjugal bed.

This way Will Carney had the use of her with none of the rest of it.

Serena never seemed to expect, nor did she demand, any outward sign of love, either physical or mental, from Will. Will was sure that Serena had accepted the idea, had resigned herself to his love, to submitting to his wants or desires. He could tell by the way she looked at him, by the expression on her face when he came into the room, but he never had quite the courage to test her for it.

And Serena never brought it up.

Perhaps because she already had him again and again in her dreams.

Inside the van it was as dark as a cave. The light of the work lamp, hooked to the dashboard in the cab, merely created an oblong of ochre glow. It made a pale nimbus of Serena's hair. It seemed to gather light where there was no light. For the rest, a detail here and there was picked out. Paulette, her huge bulk jammed tight among fallen boxes and bales, was seen, in her white sail of a dress, only as a very slightly paler gray against gray velvet.

Paulette was crying steadily, more in embarrassment than fear, for having wet herself. She was fastidious about her personal self, allowing no least soil or stain to mar her huge body. It was the greatest portion of her pride, as well.

"Stop your crying, Paulette, please," Colonel John said in a surprisingly deep and vibrant voice. It echoed in the van, sounding good to his own ears, strong, masculine and, he hoped, without a trace of fear. In the dark, no one hearing his voice would imagine him a midget.

"Did you take your . . . Have you taken your . . . Have you relieved yourself, Paulette?" Serena asked, her mind confused by the jumbled emotions that Paulette projected. It seemed an unkind question but was not meant as such.

Paulette began to weep anew.

Serena tried to reach out to her in the gloom, tried to push a hazy, comforting dream to Paulette across the narrow confines of the wrecked truck—in fact, to each of them, but the accident had unnerved her and her powers seemed to have waned.

"Damn it, enough! You mustn't cry any more, sweet Paulette," said Colonel John, not at all unkindly. He reached up to rap on the window to the cab but it was too high for him and he, like Paulette, was walled in and trapped by dangerously balanced goods.

"Can you reach the window, Serena?" he asked.

Serena moved what little she could, and Colonel John could see her a bit better in the light. She raised her arm and the whiteness of it floated in the air like a length of ectoplasm risen from the spirit world. Her fingers moved and trembled, a white sea anemone, a five-fingered sea creature from the lightless depths, sensitive and alert, sensing the very vibrations in the air.

Her delicate fingers absorbed the infinitesimal heat cast by the yellow work light. Her fingers reached the window and drummed lightly upon it.

"Can it be forced open? Can we break through it, my dear?" the Colonel asked, his face hidden in the dark.

"It's very thick," she said, fearing that they could not.

"What the hell are you doing?" Will Carney shouted from the cab, startled by the taps on the window. "Are we playing goddamn games?"

"We need some light back here," Colonel John shouted back. "We have to see if we're to get out of here at all."

"Stay right where you are! You bloody little maniac! Don't move! Don't do anything!"

"But Will," began Colonel John, "unless we . . ."

"Someone will come for us! But if you damn well move, you'll send us to our deaths, sure as sin." There was raw, naked fear in Will's voice.

Colonel John frowned, trying to shift his small frame

against the weights resting against them. He was able to move only a little. "Perhaps Will is right. Perhaps moving would be dangerous. We'll wait."

It sounded like a death sentence from an unrelenting judge.

What they would wait for was not clear. They were on an old, abandoned road, long out of use, miles from anyone. No one would come, or if they did, more likely it would be only to find their bodies in the wrecked truck at the bottom of the ravine.

Serena turned and stared back at the freaks tumbled amid the wreckage and clutter inside the truck, seeing them with her sightless eyes, her remarkable fingers. Her mind touched Marco's mind as he sat silently in the cab, slowly bleeding his life away. She felt the gentle rush and flow of life ebbing in his veins. Marco's mind seemed remarkably clear, clearer than it had ever been in her memory. He seemed to have found some peace in himself that she felt was his growing acceptance of approaching death.

Her mind probed each of them in turn, Pepino the Rubber Man, Colonel John, and Paulette. She probed Will Carney's mind, reading the terror, larger in his mind than in all the others, for death was something that robbed him of all his dignity.

And in this reading of them, she sought the key to open the door that would set them all free. She probed deep within them, past their hopes and wants and bodily needs, to their dreams, to the primal streams that made them all tick.

Each and every one of them had become infected with a kind of stunned paralysis, an inability to act or move. To move was to court death, to move wrongly was to wed it.

And so, in dreams resigned to the idea of death, they

were content to do nothing until the rain washed enough of the mountain out from under the wheels and made the decision for them.

There is a wrongness in this, this stupid and ugly death. None of them wanted to die. It was a thought in each mind she probed. Serena could not sit back and let them go quietly and unprotestingly to their deaths. She might not be able to help, they might all still die, but she meant for them all to fight against it.

Serena wrapped her hands against her chest, as if drawing her body physically within herself. She had to concentrate, she had to reach them all in some way.

She dreamed the strongest dream she had ever dreamed in her life and it went out into the night and into them all, touching them all.

The fear in Will's mind, the utter stark terror, repelled her. His mind was past all reason and her dream was closed out. The other freaks had terror in keeping with their diminished stature in the world and they opened their minds to her, unknowingly, and she began the dream for them, trying to make them see as she saw, dream as she dreamed.

It was her secret and her power.

She understood them all, what made each of them what they were, their hopes, fears, cowardices, and petty acts. And knowing them false, she loved them anyway. For the pain. She loved them for the pain. And she lived for that moment when she would wrench them out of this lifetime, and in so doing, make them strong until the end came that made death love them.

And because she understood them, she gave them each a dream promise in keeping with each of the kinds of pain each of them lived.

Pepino the Rubber Man she reached first, and she made him two promises, both terrible in their own way.

Very terrible.

And only that, because they were true.

Pepino was a philosopher and had always been one. He examined the ways of the world like a scientist counting drops of blood in the teeming cells of a corpse.

He knew himself to be mediocre. Even his double-jointedness, which set him apart from most of the world, had no drama to it.

From the first day he bent his thumb back to his forearm for the amusement of his schoolmates, his antic talent was little better than commonplace. After all, there was Harriet down the block, who'd been born with a sixth toe on each foot, and Martin, who could spit clear across the width of the boys' john. There were special wonders as fine or finer than his own.

He did have, however, the advantage of having been born a gypsy, and was trained from the beginning in the technique of making coin from even such meager gifts as his own.

He lived with the woman he thought to be his mother in a storefront in Philadelphia. A constantly changing gypsy family of between twenty and thirty shared the space with him. He found that pleasant for several reasons.

He was never without companionship or confederates
in games or ventures of small thievery. He had partners in
sexual experimentation and lost his virginity to a cousin—
he supposed that was what she was—when he was twelve.
There was always more than enough shared warmth in his
nighttime bed to keep him comfortable in the coldest of
Philadelphia winters. Even the fact that some of the
younger children of the protean family occasionally relieved themselves upon his own body during the night,
only served to teach him humility and forbearance, useful
tools for a philosopher.

The jumble of children served as cover for his frequent
truancy from public school. He stopped going altogether
sometime around the sixth grade. He found his education
for himself at the public library and never stole a book
from it, much as he would have liked to.

There was one great unpleasantness. He rarely had
enough to eat. His appetite was abnormal. Thin as a rail,
some furnace within his belly consumed food in great
quantity and left almost nothing upon his bones.

His life, all of his life, had been one long battle to keep
the pangs of hunger stilled.

He joined his first carnival on the promise that he would
be given all the hot dogs, sausages, candy, and popcorn he
could eat. If he spent everything he earned on food, he
still did not get enough.

Pepino learned in time to manipulate his body so that
he "grew" four inches by simply stretching his elastic
frame. He amused the crowds by scratching his back with
his own foot. He made his stomach "disappear" by drawing it in till his belly button very nearly touched his back-
bone. He learned never to smile while he performed such
outrageous and ludicrous acts and that served to make the
crowds laugh boldly at his otherwise rather unattractive
antics.

His skills were altogether unstartling and, somehow, more sad than ultimately amusing. They were largely unsalable, as well. Double-jointed rubber men were plentiful if not exactly a drug on the market.

He earned his keep by being a jack-of-all-trades, but since everyone in carnivals and circuses was adept at many skills, he was not the only jack-of-all-trades traveling in his circle and therefore, once more, was a commonplace.

He had long, slender, and clever fingers, and shared out with his employers the bounty of the pockets he sometimes picked. It was not a happy skill for a philosopher and he did it only when his enormous appetite gave him little choice.

He was an excellent shill. When the hicks were lured to the games of chance by his imaginary but loudly proclaimed winnings, he would smile widely and the sudden, extraordinary gladness that illuminated his face seemed a benediction and a guarantee that his good fortune should be their own.

Even so, smiling was no great pleasure to him. He considered it to be a refutation of all that he knew to be true about life. His summation of life, of its meaning and being, was a simple and direct but profound one: no one would ever have his or her appetite satisfied completely.

Life meant one was born to suffer hunger eternally until released by death.

Pepino marked the quality of his friends by the size of their appetites and the degree to which they were able to still them.

The Colonel, when first they'd met, had impressed him with his overwhelming, all-encompassing, appetite to be tall, threatening, powerful, and, sadly, even potent with large women. It underlaid the midget's every action—his

great dreams, day and night, of large things welcoming
his potency.

Marco the Strong Man hungered after a place on the
crowded earth to call his home. He was, therefore, a
lonely wanderer on the face of it, pretending that he had
such a dwelling place for the heart back in a fairy-tale land
called Newark, New Jersey.

Fat Paulette wanted love served in many flavors in a
crystal boat. Food was love and so her mouth was a small,
pursed cherry and her breasts were mounds of whipped
cream. She was a child without hope for love, for true
love, Pepino knew. Her love was as silly as a dripping ice-
cream cone.

Pepino knew real love was a serious matter, an im-
mense thing, jealous and twisted and devious, hard to find
and even harder to keep.

Pepino, like all the others, was drawn to Serena.

In the moon child, he saw a hunger so vast that it might
devour the entire universe were it ever given the means
and leave to do so.

Hers was a frightening appetite, hidden behind blind
eyes and a soft, smiling, innocent mouth.

Pepino loved her and was glad that she was not beautiful in all parts of herself. Otherwise, he would have served
himself up to her as a sacrifice.

But Pepino was enchanted most of all by Will Carney,
for in him he saw the rudest, most blatant appetite of all.
The man was glossy and modern, cheap and inept, brassy
and hopeful, boastful, vain, frightened, bloody-minded,
and cowardly. Yet, he wanted to live. His appetite was not
alone for the particulars of life but for life itself.

It was this hunger that Pepino admired and envied. He
had no such desire for life himself but his philosopher's
soul chided and abused him for not desiring it. His mouth

told him that death was a dry bone, yet he had a taste for it.

With all such dark, Romany contemplation, he was, nevertheless, considered a fairly jolly companion. He never told anyone that, when he smiled into his or her face, he saw death's head there.

He had been with Will Carney longer than most of the others. He had, from time to time, considered that he would probably be with Will still when all the others were dead and gone away.

Now, it would seem, as he lay trapped in the darkness in the back of the truck, they would all leave one another and the world in one moment. In a feast of death.

Would his hunger then be stilled?

Serena seized upon his hunger then, in a dream, and fed him.

Cooked, carved, and put upon a platter before him, she offered up her own flesh.

She was a thousand flavors and tastes on his tongue. She was every morsel of food he had ever eaten or wanted in his lifetime. Her arms, the delicate meat around her neck and chest, was a delicacy that almost ripped his soul out of his body.

The dream tantalized.

He hungered.

In the dark, trapped in her dream, he wept, aching for the forbidden taste, for that thing that seemed to promise an end to hunger, an end to a lifetime of wanting.

Serena shuddered, feeling his teeth upon her skin in the dream, feeling the marrow sucked so deliciously out of her thin, birdlike bones, the little legs she offered him, as sweet to eat as roasted larks, a delight beyond the known pleasures of this world. She was a feast for him that no king, no rich man had ever seen on this earth, nor would ever see.

She awoke the great and terrible hunger of his life.

Then, in one offering of herself, she promised to still it for all time, to sate him of his terrible need.

All this, the dream promised him, awaits you if you escape, the feast is yours if you act, move, awake.

That was the first terrible promise.

The second was the reality that awaited them all. Pepino felt the truck shake, shudder, the lurch sickeningly outward and down. A great thunderous roaring tore at his ears and his chest. The truck plummeted downward.

Bones broke through his skin, shattering against each other inside his body. The truck spun end over end.

There his hand was crushed, there his legs broken, and finally at the bottom, a great bursting and sundering which eviscerated him. He lay in a pool of his own blood, his chest torn open, his insides threatening to fall out.

That was only a part of the horror she made him see.

For as Pepino lay there, she made him feel, yes, hungry. Ravenous.

And the dream promised it for an eternity after death.

Pepino stirred, the dream of only a few seconds' duration, gleaming like summer lightning in his mind.

Gone was the paralysis, the terror that had overcome mind and muscles.

In the same way, with different dreams and promises, she touched Paulette and Colonel John. In Colonel John she found the leader, the one they must obey if they were to escape.

Her dream washed across the midget's mind, a tidal surge that moved deep inside his mind. Colonel John stiffened suddenly in the dark, as if electric currents had passed through his body. He felt great things suddenly astir in the night, things that swam in the flow of his own blood up the dark creeks of his brain. He seemed to travel elsewhere, to a land beneath a star-pricked sky. He put his head out into that night and looked up at the sickle moon only to find two instead of one.

Comets of iridescent red and blue flashed in the sky above him. Earthquakes rocked the ground gently beneath his feet in a strange, almost tribal, surration.

White rime spun a delicate mist over the grass and, turning his head, he saw the great forest from which it seemed he had just come. It was an enchanted land of silvers and golds and rich greens and towering growths of crystal like great frozen fires.

And then ahead of him, some great and wondrous beast moved and he turned to see it move past him in full flight. And his eyes went wide in astonishment, in unabashed wonder, for it was a beast of fable, a night legend, a unicorn of silver and gray and beautiful in its being.

And as it passed by, its silver mane brushed against him and burned his face, a delicious witch-cool heat. And the legs that had been too short, grew.

The arms that were like toy appendages stretched out. Like Alice, he grew and grew, each part of him advancing with perfect symmetry, until he stood, a handsome, whole man in the glare of the two moons above his head.

It was a wonder so big his heart seemed fit to burst from his chest. And so he reached out, trying to move his body to the rhythm of the dream. His body coursed with a new energy, a confidence regained. For him the dream never withered, never died and in so doing left him changed, the leader, the decider of their fate.

For Serena had dreamed Colonel John into a giant and he now felt himself to be one.

Paulette was the hardest to reach and the easiest to console. Serena smiled at her in the dark; her hands trembled, her sightless eyes blinked with tears. The smile was replaced by a sudden look of pain. The strain of the effort

Serena was making was beginning to tell on her fragile little misshapen body.

Paulette gasped as she sensed Serena's dream thrusting into her consciousness. The shock of it almost pushed her into hysteria. It was so sudden, so overwhelming, she felt as if she was going mad.

But Serena, ever soothing, ever gentle, with pleasing fragments of the dream, reached deep within Paulette and won her over with a dream bigger even than Paulette herself.

Serena pushed and pulled and delicately scissored at the dream until it most kindly reached Paulette's secret self. Paulette was appeased and settled back into the beauty of the offered dream. It was a dream so completely tailored out of Paulette's desires and inmost thoughts that it had a meaning only she could embrace.

In this dream Paulette dove into a dark pool. She went down deeper and deeper, toward death, it seemed, but the farther beneath the surface of the water, the lighter she seemed to get, as if the mounds of fat, the huge shivering bulk of her, disappeared into nothingness. Less and less she weighed, until she became something she had never been, until she became the girl she had always seen in her eyes but had never found.

She was thin now, with sparkling eyes and alabaster skin. She could dance and leap, and she could run faster than the unicorn. Oh yes, he was there in the dream, too. And Paulette stood beside Colonel John, in his dream a man now grown, and they held hands in the silver of the moonlight and her voice joined his in calling for the ones they loved.

Escape. That was the word that seemed to echo through the dream. The wind through the strange forest seemed to whisper that one word.

Escape.

Glum Pepino, the Romany who suffered for all, the Rubber Man, moved out of the forests of night and his voice joined theirs, his mind sang in their hearts. It was a very real touching, this movement of dream in the dark. Their minds, when seized, stirred as if prodded by electricity. Their hearts raced and sweat formed on their foreheads. As gentle as their shared dream was, it somehow exacted a terrible toll for their bodies, contorted in the grip of some great and terrible pain.

Escape.

And the dream went ever on, changing. Now it was a part of Colonel John's dream and now it was a part of Paulette the Fat Woman's dream. Pepino rushed into their dream night, his life spilling at their feet in a pool of reproach and interrupted sleep. Always hungry, that had been Pepino's lot, hungry as much in mind as in body, and in this shared dream world where they all traveled, Pepino found Eden. He found a world where all he saw or touched could be eaten. The sky itself was candy. Pepino was a black bear, fat in the beginning of winter, once honey-hungry, now sated because he had eaten the autumn moon. Beside Colonel John the Giant and Paulette, a beautiful woman/girl, sleek and quick as a gazelle, Pepino became full beyond measure because life came rushing at him in an overwhelming swoop. He feasted in an instant on every bit and morsel of it. A bit of the moon, a slice of the sky, all bursting with hunger, destroying beauty on his tongue.

Oh yes, and the unicorn danced for him, too. And they were all joined in a dream until it reached back for the loveliest one of them all, blind, horribly deformed, Serena. She moved in her own dream, and even as she moved in it, she gave herself, out of kindness, a small portion of wishes she could never have, her own, sometimes terrible, needs.

The dream moved in colors and hues that had long since left Serena except as memories. The unicorn came galloping toward them from the emerald green forest. Its eyes were deepest sea blue, its mane the gold and silver fire of the sun. On its back was a rainbow with colors the world had yet to see. All the things in the dark that only her fingers had sensed, suddenly reemerged into a golden, shining light. She saw through her eyes, many-eyed, many-sighted, and her heart was touched and she led them through the dream.

Their bodies became as one. To act, to do, to move as one, finally, to escape, to go to the dreamworld Serena promised them life could yet be. That was the promise that grew and grew, getting so strong in their minds that their bodies strained under the very weight of it. Their hearts raced, a fever raged in their blood, hotter and hotter. The air rattled in struggling chests. The dream grew and their own fears, their sense of helplessness, diminished in its path.

The bright dreamland beckoned them the last step, the final commitment to the dream of doing, acting as one.

To escape the final black oblivion of death.

Such glory they had in this loving, this shared dream.

The Strong Man moved, his elbow smashing heavily into the door panel, forgetting for the moment his great strength. The truck shook with the sound of metal straining against metal. The truck quivered like some great wounded beast in its death throes. The dream deserted them like a light going out.

Pepino, the dark sentimentalist, stared in agony at the floor. "We must . . . I feel a new life within our grasp. We . . ." The import of the great dream still overwhelmed him.

They were all other than they had been. Serena's pale hand sought and found Colonel John's shoulder. She touched him gently. Her unseeing eyes were on the midget, who was tense, almost in a benumbed state, a kind of awe at the awful power he now felt thrust upon him.

Serena met Colonel John's eyes. "I'm sure, if we wish it, we can all go to a new life, we can find a way out of here."

The midget licked his lips. He shrugged his shoulders, as if dropping a burden. "I'm sure of it," he told her, telling all of them. "Now that I know the way. We *will* go!"

The colonel squared his shoulders.

"Touch the window again, Serena," he said, his voice booming authoritatively in the darkened van.

She did so, tapping lightly on the pane.

Will cried out, "Don't! Be Still! Don't you dare move back there."

Colonel John laughed. "If that's the strategy of it, we might as well say the Requiem Mass right now because the rain will soon wash us away."

"Wait!" Will Carney was close to panic.

"What are you planning to do?" asked Pepino.

"We've got to break through the window," said Colonel John.

"No!" That was Will.

"Nevertheless," said Colonel John. "Will, find me something to hammer at the window with, something Marco can use to batter at the glass with."

Will, never strong, gave in. He looked at the opened glove compartment. He reached over and tapped Marco on the shoulder. Marco opened his eyes, sighing with pain. Will gestured toward the screwdriver, then pantomimed a smashing action with his hand toward the window behind his head. Marco nodded that he understood and then reached forward. The screwdriver was hardly suitable. Still, it was the nearest thing to a bludgeon they had. His arms were getting stiff. He tried to raise his arm, to swing the screwdriver back at the window, but he was unable to move. The pain was terrible.

He handed the screwdriver over to Will.

"Can Marco smash out the window?"

Will held the screwdriver tightly in his hand, his sweat making the wooden grip clammy. "Marco can't lift his arms. He's been shot."

The group in the back of the truck was stunned. They had not known, except for Serena. Serena had felt the gunshot wound as deeply as if she herself had been shot.

"How bad is it?" cried Colonel John.

"It's bad," said Will.

"Is it . . . ? Does he . . . ?"

"You ask me, I think he's dying," said Will. "There's a lot of blood. The poor devil's had it, I'm afraid."

Colonel John's head sank on his chest, his eyes closing and unclosing, a single tear edging his eye. Paulette, still weeping softly in the dark, wept anew, a little this time for friend Marco. Only Pepino seemed unmoved but that was only an appearance.

"Can you do it, then, Will?" asked Colonel John, and his voice cracked with sudden emotion.

Settling himself for the effort, Will tried to turn in the seat. The axle beneath them set up a slender rasp, as if shifting, and Will froze in place.

He was paralyzed, unable to think how to move or act. Serena felt this in Will and quickly, in a swiftly thought dream, tried to image for him what he himself was too frightened to see.

His fear was so great, and his mind, as always, so hard to reach, behind that ever-shifting mask of lies and illusion, that little of what she thought at him seeped through to him. But a little did, enough at any rate, that he lifted his arm, his hands clumsily holding the screwdriver.

He could not strike over his shoulder with his right

hand. He transferred the screwdriver to his left, to the maimed hand, and gripped it as best he could. He struck tentatively, swinging across his chest. The handle of the screwdriver made no mark on the window glass and the tool was wrenched from his hand. It fell upon the seat, bounced, and landed on the floor.

Marco, sensing what was needed, bent forward to retrieve the screwdriver. The axle or some other part of the cab's structure screamed again, metal grinding against stone.

"What are you doing up there? What are you doing?" Colonel John yelled to Will.

"It's no use. I tried to break the glass so I could pass the work lamp through, but we can't move up here. The slightest move will send us over."

"Well, hold the lamp up to the window, at least. Give us as much light as you can."

Will stared at the work lamp fixed to the dashboard. It was only a bent waist and an arm's length away but he was desperately afraid to reach for it. Marco watched him. Suddenly, casually and without any caution at all, he reached over and took it. There was no further shifting of the rig. Marco smiled as he handed Will the lamp, smiled as though he were telling Will he was a coward.

Will held the lamp up to the window.

It offered light to the interior of the van now. Colonel John could see how badly off they all were. Serena, against the bulkhead of the cab, was the freest, though her tiny legs were encumbered by coils of tent rope. Paulette shook, with the repression of her sobs, down near the tailgate. She was half leaning upon, half supported by, a welter of tumbled boxes, footlockers, and bales of goods. The extent of her imprisonment was still unclear in the feeble light.

Pepino was wound around with poles and canvas rigging. He seemed now like a spider trapped in its own web.

The colonel himself was held in a kind of small cave of many things. "Is there a heavy tool or iron bar close to your hand, Pepino?"

The Rubber Man extricated one arm and felt all about in front and to the side and far behind him in the places no normal man could cast his hand. A smile illuminated his dark face as he dragged forth a heavy pry bar.

"Can you reach far enough with it to crack the window glass?" asked Colonel John.

Pepino tried, stretching out his arm to the limit of his curious skill. The truck shook and seemed to rock gently. Pepino recovered his place.

"Serena can reach it from where she sits, I think," Pepino said. He handed the pry bar first to Colonel John. It was very heavy, but he held it in one hand and felt very powerful. He passed it across to Serena. He feared, as he did so, it would be too much weight for the fragile moon child to bear.

"Reach out your hand and take the metal bar from me," he said. "Don't be afraid."

"I'm not afraid. Just tell me what to do," she said and laughed a little. It was a strangely happy sound.

"The window to the cab has to be broken. You'll have to do it. We need more light in here," said Colonel John anxiously.

"Yes, light," said Serena, with her own meaning to it, and she swung the heavy bar unerringly at the window. The blow landed with surprising force. The glass turned milky with starring. Colonel John gasped in admiration.

"And again, my little love," said Colonel John with pride.

She swung again and again. Bits of glass fell to the floor. Again and again. Broken shards fell inside the cab, as well.

Finally, the chicken wire embedded in the glass was cleared, bent but still intact.

They seemed suddenly to become aware that Will was screaming at them in a voice that was a siren-loud keen. "Stop it! We'll go over! You'll kill me! Stop! Stop!"

The truck had shifted not an inch and had made no protest. But in Will's mind it had given a great lurch with each blow. Actually, Serena, as she swung the bar, was at that perfect point of balance that a hundred engineers never could have plotted.

"Now for the chicken-wire mesh," Colonel John said, delighted with the progress they had made. He reached into his pocket and managed to bring out the clippers with which he trimmed his nails. He handed it across to the blind girl. "Can you reckon how this works?" he asked.

She manipulated the little tool in the finger of one hand, immediately divining its usefulness. She set it properly to lever the cutting blades, and, reaching up as before—when she'd first touched the glass—she snipped away at the wire.

Snip. Snip. Snip.

The nail trimmer made a cricket like sound. Soon a space was made.

In the cab, Marco, perhaps feeling the vibrations, had turned slightly in his seat, until he could see the hole taking shape in the window. Serena worked industriously at the wire. It was slow going, as the wire resisted the rapidly dulling blades.

With a silent grunt of pain, Marco forced his arm up until his hand closed on the gap in the mesh. His fingers gripped the mesh and he fell back, using his weight as much as his muscles to pull it free from the window.

Will moved then, thrusting the lamp through into the van. Serena grasped it, led to it by the heat of the bulb, and handed it down to the Colonel. He in turn gave it over to Pepino, who held it high over his head midway along the length of the van.

The Colonel could see well, now. It was clear to him that Paulette was not so badly trapped as she believed she was. There was a puddle of wet at her feet. In the light, she stared at him with her small currantlike eyes suddenly grown wide and round in her thick pudding of a face.

"Paulette, my love, move your left arm very, very slowly. If that box holds on top of the one beneath it, half of you will be free," the Colonel urged.

"I'm afraid," she whimpered.

Serena sent a warm, comforting thought at her, trying to ease the fear that choked her.

Colonel John blinked in the light. "Such a big girl," he soothed, and there was no drollery in his words. "Come along and give it a try. There's nothing, my big darling, to be afraid of."

She stood or lay there, quivering with fright, unable to make that first tentative move.

"Come along now, my little roly-poly, my little cushion of perfume." It sounded silly in the dark and that was how he meant it. She so loved things that were silly.

"Come along, my pretty cake of French cheese. My little apple-cheeked darling. Would I suggest you do anything to harm yourself?"

Serena's thoughts had no effect on Paulette but Colonel John's silly words reached her. She giggled. She could not resist absurd endearments. She moved her mountain of an arm and nothing tumbled down about her.

"There! You see!" said Colonel John triumphantly. "You're quite safe. Now, my little goose, move your other arm."

Paulette moved again and the van trembled. She screamed and cried out. "I'm going to faint!"

"If you do, and cause us to fall, I'll never kiss your pretty cheeks again. And you know you'll get no better kisses elsewhere." It sounded comical, this strange threat he made, and it worked. He laughed softly in the dark and it was the thing that kept Paulette from going over. The Colonel laughed, although fear was like a hand at his own throat.

Serena smiled. She admired the little man's courage and even more, the depth of his understanding and love of those around him. Only by making light of it, by playing it for laughs, could he still Paulette's fears. It was a stroke of genius, the way he kept her sane, for, despite her great size, in some ways, Paulette was the most fragile of them all.

Paulette giggled in spite of herself. He did have the sweetest way about him, did Colonel John.

"Keep moving, my wondrous jelly roll. Move ever so slowly toward the back of the truck, now there's my love," said Colonel John, sweat dripping off his face.

Pepino stared at Paulette as a hare is transfixed by the gaze of a snake. Serena stared into her private dark and smiled softly. She alone of them, felt no fear. What, after all, had she to fear? While it lasted, it was adventure, it was time and motion and life and death, intensified a hundred times and made larger than all things in creation. If it ended in death for her, it did not concern her. She cared only about the others, about their living or dying. As for herself, it would be, if she met death here, only a going from one darkness to another.

Paulette moved back, slowly, inch by inch.

"Once more, Paulette, my little sugar bun."

Paulette moved, drawing back until she was completely unencumbered, and everything stayed in place—boxes, baggage, trunks, and all. If the truck settled at all, it was in a positive direction, the front of it lifting up as she moved to the back.

"Oh, what a delight you are. Now you've gone as far back as you can go. Just a little more, my love. Spread your feet, balance yourself carefully. Then edge over, move inch by inch to the side of the truck farthest from you, to the side closest to the mountain wall. Are your feet firmly on the floor?"

"Yes."

"Move as slowly as a snail, my love."

She moved, stopping for a second when the metal of the truck cried in warning.

"I can't go on."

"You must or we're done for. Move or we're dead."

She gasped and the Colonel could imagine her heart beating in the great, ice-cream mound of her. He knew the risk in frightening her so. She might well have made some sudden, fateful move in a terrified attempt to escape the death he warned her of. But he had no choice. He could no longer mask his own fear. This threat of death was his only play. But she did not panic and he was glad he had taken the hard line.

"Don't move! In the name of God, don't move!" Will screamed in that desperate way that was more a whisper than a loud cry.

"Do it, Paulette," the Colonel demanded in a strong, unforgiving voice. "In the name of the Juggler." The last remark was a subtle and sardonic one meant to sting Will Carney. In the use of the sarcastic phrase, so often used by Will to explain the reason for all things that were done, fair or unfair, the Colonel did, as well, emphasize to Paulette that she was one of the freaks in a small and special fraternity. It brought her back to herself.

Paulette laughed. It was a fierce, trapped, almost hateful sound.

She moved her tiny feet, one tiny, tiny step after another, until she was brought up short by a large trunk on the grounded side of the van.

"That's good enough. Sit down now, love," the colonel praised. "What a wonder you are! What a special wonder! You have saved us from our most immediate of dangers! You may well have bought for us the very time we need to reckon our way out of this mess."

The great burden of Paulette's life had become, in this moment, their temporary salvation.

Paulette smiled secretly and dimpled her many chins.

Paulette was billed on the side of the van as the "HUMAN PACHYDERM" and that most often drew derisive taunts. Of all the freaks, perhaps Paulette drew the bitterest and least respectful regard.

A midget was somehow cute, childlike. A moon child, a rubber man with changing symmetry, the mighty muscular grace of Marco, all these things, in their way, suggested some kind of beauty, some kind of dignity that poor Paulette was denied.

She was often driven to tears by crude insults and lewd and suggestive remarks. It was a terrible torment to her but Will Carney pointed out to her that the casting of such insults pleased the rubes and brought in the silver, sure enough. Still and all, her feelings were terribly hurt.

On the large canvas banner that was her own among

those set up on poles to form their three-sided tent, she was otherwise described as "the girl who was so fat it took six grown men just to hug her."

She was girlishly pleased by that.

Paulette was conceived in Spearman, Ochiltree County, Texas, on May 7, 1945.

On that day, V-E Day, her mother, Janine Howard, had traveled with two girl friends from their hometown of Booker, on the Oklahoma border, to the larger town for what celebration of victory it might afford.

There were some service and supply troops from a nearby depot raising Cain, flasks on their hips and campaign caps tipped so far over their eyes that they had to hold their heads back to keep from tripping over their own exaggerated senses of self-importance.

They were barracks troops, most none too bright, who'd have fainted if ever a shot was fired. But they were all brave boys that day, kissing the girls and accepting the hearty backslaps of the townspeople, who maybe saw in them the surrogates of their own sons, many of whom would never come back from the war.

Paulette's mother, Jannine, was a smaller version of Paulette, perhaps a blueprint of what Paulette herself was to become.

Janine was about five feet tall. In grade school they called her "Pint." By the time she made high school, she'd graduated to "Quart," and now that she was out on an expedition to comfort the troops, she was practically a "Gallon."

Despite her size, Janine, everyone said, was as pretty as a valentine. Her skin was cream and rose, even though there was too much of it. Janine was orphaned at seventeen. She slept with her first boy when she was eighteen.

She worked as a cook and housekeeper on a small ranch. That gave her the chance to do what she liked best. Mostly eat.

If liking to eat is a hereditary trait, Janine certainly had enough of the trait to pass on to Paulette.

On V-E Day, the soldiers found her a delight. She had other qualities besides being pleasingly overplump. She giggled more than she talked and that made the young warriors think they were mighty smart, and, swept away with the great tidal wave of V-E Day exultation, she was overly willing and that made the young soldiers feel mighty bold.

When Janine's pregnancy announced itself, she felt half proud despite the fact that she couldn't name the father.

"Just got carried far, far away that day. That V-E Day. That Victory Day," she'd often say. "All those handsome boys in their smart uniforms. A body just felt she *had* to thank them for risking their lives and young limbs to save us . . . to save America."

In that haphazard sort of way, Paulette gained entry to the world.

Paulette was born prematurely in the thirtieth week of gestation. She weighed scarcely a pound, but Janine, who herself loved to eat, saw to it that her own infant was taught the wonder.

The family cow grew thin trying to provide enough milk and Paulette grew fat.

When they got around to celebrating Paulette's tenth birthday, they celebrated her two hundreth pound as well.

About that time, out of nowhere, a tall, skinny hog raiser named Sunday Pastor—people are humorous with names in some parts of Texas—came courting and up and married Janine.

Sunday raised the biggest, whitest hogs in all Ochiltree County. They had pink snouts and rosy rings for eyelids.

Janine didn't have any more kids. On poundage alone, didn't they already have a big family?

Sunday Pastor was a man who liked fat things. That was for certain. His wife and stepchild didn't get any leaner under his roof.

When they went to the Ochiltree County Fair each year, Sunday Pastor was as proud as a kid with a new willow whistle. One year—the year Paulette was fifteen— Sunday lost first prize in the hog show to a gentleman farmer (who was no gentleman) from the East who'd rung in some champion ringers.

The gossiper type of folks said that after the judging was done and the blue ribbon pinned on a pig larger than his own, Sunday Pastor looked at his stepdaughter with a speculative eye, as though he'd like to have entered her for the judging instead. Folks added unkindly that she would have won.

She weighed three hundred pounds, after all.

Medical men say that obesity has to do with inherited body type. Both Janine and Paulette were endomorphic. They also say that overweight patients are very responsive to the availability of food. In other words, if the food's on the table, they'll eat it. That seems logical enough.

There's another villain in the piece: the hypothalamus. It's a little gland buried deep in the brain. One part of it is the appetite center and the other the satiety center. One part says "Eat." The other part says "Don't eat." This whole complex is called the appestat. When it malfunctions, it adds to the problem.

Sunday Pastor's family didn't know a thing about appestats but they knew a hell of a lot about apple pie, well-sugared and swimming in creamery butter. They knew about lard on bread with a bit of salt, pork chops, and thick rich cow's cream by the pitcher.

By the time she was seventeen, Paulette had grown into immensity. Paulette was the local wonder.

Sunday Pastor died of a fever on a Friday of that year and so got to be buried on his name day.

Janine, unable to tend the farm herself, sold it off, allowing as how she'd always hated the smell of pigs. With the proceeds, she and Paulette moved into the big city of Borger. Out on the road leading to it, the widow opened up a truckers' café.

It was the kind of business both Janine and Paulette found ideal. It was after all, involved with eating.

It was there Will Carney found Paulette as he was traveling the Southwest in a 1959 panel truck, with the back filled with junk jewlery and ladies' cotton drawers.

It wasn't love or lust that stirred Will at the sight of Paulette sitting by the soda-pop cooler fanning herself with a cardboard Coca-Cola fan. It was something more insidious. It was ambition.

He'd meant to pay for his hamburger and greasy beans with a display of juggling, if he could wangle it. But he slyly put on his usual show and when his money was waved away—as he intended—at their pleasure in it, he insisted on paying all the same.

Will Carney stayed eleven days in Borger and gave a

display of skill each morning, noon, and night, much to the delight of Janine, Paulette, and the truckers who happened by. It was a calculated performance. His hands were clever as they tossed rubber balls or paper cups or saucers, even catsup bottles and spoons, into the air above his head. But even more clever were the plans that he juggled in his head.

When he left Borger, Texas, he took Janine's twenty-four-year-old daughter, Paulette, with him and a cheery promise to keep her safe and pure, to see that she never wanted for what to eat or where to sleep or the means to care for herself and, too—of course, since that was the final selling point—he promised to send a check home to Janine once a month.

It was the check once a month to Janine that was the certified clincher.

As to his promises, Will kept her safe as he could, times being what they were. She was still pure, and unhappy for it, for she knew that people—men and women—did certain things together—he-ing and she-ing as she called it—that were a great delight and denied to her. She didn't always eat all she wanted and there were even days when there was nothing to eat at all. Will protected his investment, when he could, by stuffing her with cheap candy, but she did at times sorely miss her mother's cooking. Paulette slept sometimes, sitting up under a canvas shelter or a summer tree, but that was the least of hardships, for she'd slept sitting up for some long time for the benefit of her heart. She kept herself squeaky clean, another trait her mother had passed on to her, though sometimes that meant washing herself a square yard at a time with a handcloth and a pan of water.

Will Carney never sent a damn penny back to Janine.

Sometimes Paulette wanted to go home and felt she'd had enough of the wide world, which seemed to be nothing but a series of small, dusty, mean towns. But the thought didn't last long. The truth was, she'd grown used to Will's cheery ways—at least he was cheery the first few years until his hand got busted up and he couldn't juggle worth a damn. Later, there was Serena come to join them. And then the others, all of whom accepted her for what she was in a way others had not. The longer she stayed with these people, the deeper her kinship with these strange folk grew, and the farther and farther in her mind her thoughts of home receded. Most of all, she felt a protective love for the little albino, wanting never to leave her alone and afraid of the dark.

Paulette wrote her mother from time to time. Less often as the years passed. Her mother never wrote at all. Paulette loved her mother but she had the sneakiest little suspicion that Janine was just as happy to have her gone.

It seemed that Paulette, as much as any of them, was where she was because she had no place else to go.

Colonel John Thumb had no intention of dying scattered all over a Tennessee mountain face if there was any help at all for it. He became aware that he had been breathing in long, ragged gasps as Paulette had shifted her great weight across the width of the van. His ears now caught the sound of the other's breathing with the hiss of panic in it as well.

"Well, now," he said in his perkiest voice. "We've got one leg up on the problem, as it were."

"One leg and a wonderful lot more," Pepino said, seeming to divine the reasoning behind the Colonel's little joke and making more fun with it.

The Colonel thanked Pepino with a wink of his eye.

Paulette giggled.

Serena seemed to glow in the dark like a hearth that warmed and comforted them all.

"Now, then, first things first and next things next. We must move all the baggage and welter of things away from the back door until it rests against the side of the truck nearest the mountainside," said Colonel John.

"I've got no strength for that. I'm . . . The way I move. . . . I'm awkward," she said apologetically.

"No need, no need, my little artichoke. I would have you just exactly where you are and not to move one tiniest inch."

Colonel John shifted himself a bit in his confining nest in order to crane his neck and poke his head out beyond the barrier enough to see a bit more. His action gave no tremor to the balanced mass and he was heartened by the fact.

"Don't be afraid and, whatever happens, don't move from your places or struggle to get free. I'm going to attempt to extricate myself from this mess and welter that has me hemmed in. Don't be afraid."

"You'd better damn well stay still or I'll kill you," Will grated in a voice that was, for the moment, well under control with its burden of hate and fear. "Don't do a thing until I think on it."

Serena spoke then, a thing she seldom seemed to do.

"I'm with you, Colonel John. How can I help you?"

Pepino nodded. "Me, too."

Will was enraged. "I'm warning you. You're going to kill us all with your meddling. You're not bright enough to think for yourselves. That's why I'm boss. You just shut up and settle down back there. Give me a chance to think!"

Colonel John shook his head. "This is a time for deeds. Not management."

"I'm the boss," screamed Will. "You'll do as I say or else you'll . . ." Will couldn't think of an "or else." He was losing not only control of himself but also control over his charges.

Finally, he suggested with desperation, "We must wait it out. Someone's bound to come along this road. They could hook a chain on us and steady the truck until we could get out. The thing is to sit quietly. Help will come!"

It was not a convincing argument. It sounded weak to Will even as he said it, but it did raise some doubts in the others.

Paulette was the first to voice the doubt.

"Will might be right. Maybe help will . . ."

But Colonel John would have none of it. "Is that your idea of doing something? Wait for it, wait for help we damn sure know won't come?"

Pepino agreed. "By the time someone is liable to travel this ill-used road, it would be only to find our bodies strewn at the bottom of the mountain. I say it's up to us. Colonel John has the right of it."

Serena thought affirmative thoughts in turn to Pepino, Paulette, Will, and silent Marco, who, in his pain, was past all decisions.

"Damn it!" cried Will. "I'm the one that should say how we handle this!"

The Colonel reared back his head and laughed. "Then go out the door, climb atop the cab, scoot across the roof of the van, and open the tailgate door for us."

There was a long silence. Finally, Will spoke and there was less authority in his voice.

"You damn little fool. If I tried to do that, this whole rig would tip over and go crashing down the mountain."

The Colonel smiled. "But, Will, there's nothing to it. Just go slow and easy. If you feel her start to slip, pop inside as quick as a wink." The Colonel seemed to be enjoying it, this suggestion as to how Will should save them all.

"But there's nothing for me to stand on. No place to give my feet purchase," countered Will.

"Use your hands and the strength in your arms, man," said the midget a touch impatiently. Time was pressing them all. This was no time for explanations.

"My God, you know I can't use my maimed hand. It's not got the strength of a baby's hand." There was a whine in Will's voice that made those who heard it wince in shame for his weakness.

The Colonel found in that his justification for taking over. "I forgot all about your handicap, Will," said the midget in a very gentle voice. "That lets you out of this, then, Will. With your injured hand, you can't be expected to do it."

Will sighed with relief, settling back against the seat. He felt a little better now that he had an excuse for doing nothing. He felt some of the pressure ease. Whatever happened now, it was no longer up to him. He was a cripple, after all.

"Just sit you as still as you can, Will, and let me go about this risky business. I'm small and that's a blessing. I've not much weight, so I'm suited to this and my hands and arms are strong enough to pull me along, where my legs would fail me."

The midget straightened his shoulders, as if adjusting a heavy burden, and made a funny clicking sound with his tongue as he said, "Well, I'm about to go at it. Remember what I said, stay in your places and no one panic."

Colonel John examined the barrier of things that formed a roof above his head and reckoned the one he might move with least disturbance to the others. He chose a carton containing strings of light bulbs, which he knew to be fairly light and liable to easy shifting. One or two other parcels of goods were supported upon it but, as nearly as he could judge, moving the carton would simply allow the others to slide down together to form a sturdy arch.

He braced himself against the bundle at his back and grasped the carton with his tiny hands. He heaved up slowly, with not inconsiderable strength. He applied the upward pressure with force combined with feathery delicacy. The tiniest hiss of paper against paper marked the movement of the box as he tried to slip it out from beneath the weight of the containers above it. A bit of label tape caught an edge, impeding the box's forward motion. He applied a bit more pressure and the small snag gave way all at once and the carton jerked free.

The box struck Colonel John sharply in the chest, tumbling him to the bed of the truck. The two cartons above tumbled down together and formed a bridge over his head.

A heavy trunk tumbled down on top of them, teetering on the edge of the boxes. Colonel John looked up in horror at the huge weight suspended above him. If it fell, it would surely crush the life out of him.

The truck rocked gently but held its place upon the melting earth. The trunk stopped wobbling, safe enough for the moment.

Colonel John huddled on the floor, quivering with the effort and the fear that washed over him. He was sweating profusely.

It was very quiet. No one had cried out. No one had panicked. They had obeyed his admonishment. Still, the awful strain was stamped on all their faces.

"That seemed to be a proper stack of kiddie's blocks, did it not?" laughed Colonel John, somewhat nervously.

Only Serena, dreaming in the dark, dreaming for them all, knew the courage behind Colonel John's little joke. To laugh when fear was so great, when terror colored all that he thought or did or wanted to do, was an act of profound courage. Serena saw deeply into his mind and was amazed by the strength in the little man's character.

Colonel John wiped the sweat from his face and quickly rose to his feet with the air of someone who had fallen on purpose. "This whole higgledly-piggledly mess seems to be all of a hodge-podge. Now there's a redundancy if anyone should want one. Caution is indicated. I'll certainly have to proceed with greater care. I don't suppose we have an architect or engineer among us, do we?"

He shut his mouth. He was rattling on, he knew, because he was frightened, for one thing—more than he wanted to admit to himself—and wished to delay further action, for another. His confidence was badly shaken.

"I think I can reach the handle of the trunk that fell, that nearly fell I mean," Pepino was quick to amend.

"Does it support anything else?" asked the midget.

"I don't think so. It seems free at the top of it. But its difficult to see in the gloom," said Pepino.

"I wish Serena were close enough to touch it," mused Colonel John. "It seems to me this dark is a problem only for us. Were you free, you could be our eyes. It seems you can feel the merest touch of a butterfly's wing and sense dust motes dancing in the air. That being so, perhaps you'd be able to lay your hands on this jumble of blocks and know the one that can be moved without bringing the others tumbling down."

"Shall I try to get my legs loose of these tent ropes and things around me?" asked Serena, uncomfortable in the certain knowledge that it was a thing beyond her strength alone.

"No, no. Let me see if we can get me out of this mousehole first so that I might help you."

"You're talking very funny, John. Not like yourself at all," Paulette said suddenly.

"Funny? How so, love?" said the midget, scrambling carefully forward over tumbled boxes.

"I mean all educated and fancy," said Paulette. "Important, somehow."

Colonel John winced a little at that. He chose wisely to take it as a compliment. "Why, thank you, my dear. It is the thespian in my soul. Crisis is like a spotlight. Turn it on and one feels compelled to perform."

"What the hell is going on back there? What are you doing?" screamed Will with sudden violence. His nerves were going.

"I wish Will would stop yelling at us. He takes on so and we *are* trying to find us a way out. He don't have much patience or faith in us either," said Paulette.

"Shut up, Paulette!" said Will. "Who asked you!"

But Paulette was not to be stifled. "I swear sometimes I think Will's never growed up. I think he fusses too much when he don't get his own way."

Colonel John was delighted with the comment. Will's sniping at them made it all the more difficult for them to act, undermining the midget's authority as it did.

"That's just the case. Exactly the case," the Colonel all but crowed. "Did you hear that, Will Carney? You're just a pimple-spotted boy chasing pimple-spotted girls!"

"Shut your mouth," Will said.

"Have to prove yourself, don't you, Will? Made a mess and a grand failure of your life so you have to be a success

with the ladies, isn't that so, Will? You'd have your way
with the whole female population if you could," said Colonel John.

Paulette giggled for the thrill of the thought of it.

"Bed those that are bedable and . . . and fair in the
face and form, that's for sure," Will said and then immediately regretted the words. He hadn't meant to hurt the
two women inside the van, for he'd never had anything to
do with either of them in that way.

"You're a bloody vicious dog, you are, Will," the Colonel
cackled in a manner almost pleasant. "And you are such a
winner with the ladies. Such a world-beater. You remember that last one you snared? She turned you over and
blistered you a good one, didn't she? Made you out to be
the damn bloody fool, didn't she, and her only a half-
grown pup?" The Colonel's taunts rang with irony. There
was a smile of triumph on his face. He was definitely in
control now.

Serena smiled with him, his triumph in subtle ways also
hers.

The counterman and owner of the run-down café had
roused his wife to come out and see the freaks. She peered
at them, holding a tattered, pink chenille robe about her
doughy body. Her eyes were gummy with sleep and there
was a network of ingrained dirt in the creases of her un-
washed neck. Her eyes slowly took in fat Paulette, moon

child Serena, tiny Colonel John, and the huge mountain of
Marco.

"Ain't that a sight?" she said, with an indelicate shudder. "Fitting to give a body the screaming haunts."

"Ain't scaring you, are they? You want I should send
them away?" her husband asked.

"Are they human?" she said. "They ain't spook folk, are
they? They most give me the crawling creeps!"

"They are after cadging a free meal. Reckon spook folk
don't hanker after grits and gravy," said her husband.
"Reckon they are every bit as much human as us, scroung-
ers and freaks in one package."

"Don't send them away, Pa. Please let them stay." This
came from one of the couple's young daughters, a pretty
and not too bright young thing. She eyed the freaks with
unabashed delight, her eyes wide as shiny saucers. "It's
like a circus come to visit," she said. She was scantily clad
and even at her tender age, her overdeveloped body and
bright eyes signaled trouble.

"Aw, hell. Let them stay a whiles," the wife finally
agreed. They seemed to promise the unusual and God
knew there was little enough of that in this barren place
beside the road. She called her daughters all out by name
and sent the four of them off to spread the word among
the neighbors. "Ought to make a couple heads turn, we
show people this kind of truck. Maybe bring in a few
paying customers, too, 'stead of them damn deadbeat
friends of yours," she added, her mind sensing a profit in it
all.

The neighbors and some farmers from an easy distance
all around came to gawk. They stood and stared as Marco
lifted up great chunks of scrap metal from the bodies of
old, wrecked cars dumped in mouldering heaps in the
back parking lot behind the café.

The crowd tittered and poked one another in the ribs as

Colonel John hurried about, a dish towel tied about his waist, washing the windows, sweeping the floors, and doing it all in ways that invented the means to reach where normal men might easily reach.

The women in the crowd whispered together and reached out hands stained dark as butternut to touch pale Serena's hair, as she delicately, with stitches shiny as gossamer, darned the café owner's socks and well-holed drawers. Paulette sat beside her and laughed more than she meant to. She knew these people hated her for being fat. Most people resented it even as they marveled at it, so she wanted to appear jolly so they would not think too unkindly of her.

And all this time, where was Will Carney? What was he up to? Why, in a shed behind the run-down garage with the young daughter, just old enough, barely, to have her first taste of sin. The little girl turned out to be much older than she looked, at least in her share of worldly experience. Her skill in love astonished even Will.

When her mother opened the door to the shed near on to dusk, when Will was juggling for yet another book from the daughter's shelf of experience, the daughter, wise to the ways of sin and punishment, pushed Will away. Stunned, he fell over on his back, which ached with the enthusiastic sting of sharp fingernails. The girl started shouting bloody murder and even bloodier rape.

While the old lady scrambled after her still shrieking daughter, bent on whaling the daylights out of her, for the mother was not in the least bit fooled. Will managed to run stumblingly out of reach. With a scream, he called the members of his troupe together, and, only half clad, pushed and shoved at his confused and thoroughly frightened charges until they were all back in the truck and speeding away.

In the confusion, Will's wallet, which the not-so-innocent daughter had thoughtfully removed from his trousers, was safe under the straw where she had hid it.

The tires of the truck keened as they peeled out of the roadside-café parking lot, an angry crowd railing at them as they fled. Will would have no doubts his wallet had been cleverly lifted, for to get it out at all, his pocket had to be unbuttoned. Every last dime they had in the world was in that wallet.

As they highballed down the road, Will—in the driver's seat—felt the absence in his back pocket and cursed a blue streak.

Colonel John had laughed in his face when Will had had to explain by what means the money had come to be gone. Will had been all the more furious that Colonel John had dared to laugh. He suspected they all were laughing at him behind his back. He was blind mad and stayed that way for the next three days and more. It was this girl the midget was now twitting Will about, and the reminder brought back all of Will's rage and frustration. Could he but get his hands on the little peacock of a man, he would surely wrench his neck until it popped like a cork from a bottle.

"You were lucky all she did was get your wallet. She could have given you a dose of you know what for good measure," teased the midget. Paulette laughed at the witticism. The Colonel was being quite wicked.

Will gave no answer to the Colonel's taunts. In his silence in the darkened cab, hovering on the edge of certain death, his failure to reply was a confession of his shame, his humiliation. More than anything, Will Carney could not stand to be laughed at, to not be taken seriously. It was the deepest wound of all.

"The dark gets darker and we are not much further along I think," said Serena softly, bringing them back to what was.

The Colonel nodded and backed off then, gave it over, for there was no taste in cheap victory. "That's that, then," he said, dismissing Will from his mind. There was work to be done.

"Do you want me to reach for the trunk?" Pepino asked.

"Yes," said Colonel John. "Let's try it now."

Pepino reached out his hand and loosened up the joints of the limb. It worked as smoothly as the extension on a mechanical claw. His fingers touched the leather loop on the side of the trunk. Touched but no more. He took a great gulp of air into his chest and stretched the arm out until it ached fiercely at shoulder and elbow. His fingers hooked the handle. He pulled it toward him, let the joints pull for him as they went back into place. The trunk slid free and he resettled it where it would do no harm.

The Colonel removed first one and then the other of the bundles arched above him. He struggled, like a small ferret, out of the space he was in, wriggling and feeling his way like a rodent in his burrow, making himself smaller in places as he went along.

At last, Colonel John stood free, trembling all over his small body. He felt disoriented, straightened his shoulders, feeling vaguely uncomfortable. Surely a giant was ten times taller than he felt himself to be at this moment. But he smiled. It did not quite matter. Bright remnants of Serena's wondrous dream of himself danced in back of his eyes. A giant looked out of his eyes.

Paulette clapped her hands as though Colonel John had done a trick. He waved her silent with a grand gesture and stood there, his feet planted well apart, one hand upon his hip as though upon the hilt of a sword.

He furrowed his brow, planning strategies, assessing strengths and weaknesses, a small Wellington at Waterloo or a small Napoleon on the occasion of other victories.

There was a nightmare world, dark and deadly, just outside the van, threatening death to them all. That was clearly in his mind and might have overwhelmed him with fear and an inability to act but for Serena.

Serena dreamed silently at him in the dark. Not giving him courage, not tendering strengths to him he did not have. She only dreamed inside him and discovered the great courage in his own heart, the great strength in his tiny body, and removed the fears that would have shackled him, that would not have let them happen. In this way, she saw into his secret self and let it all go free, to act and do.

Colonel John smiled at the dark of the night.

He was in command.

When Colonel John was a little boy—and there was humor in that, when he thought of that expression, because he had in some ways never quite ceased being a little boy —he remembered an old man in a park who had once terrified him. The old man sat in the park waiting for little boys who looked exactly like young John to come along, or so the old man said, at any rate.

The old man had talked very pleasantly, at first. He bade young John sit beside him on the bench which he had done with some nervousness. The old man had escaped from a circus, a white one in a huge building with many strange rooms and screaming animals in padded cages. That's how the old man described it and there was such a funny, strange quality to his voice when he said it. The old man had a brown paper bag on his lap. It was full of light bulbs, very cleverly stolen light bulbs, the old man claimed.

He drew a dusty light bulb from his sack. It was gray with age and much fly bespeckled. He offered it to young John, who backed away along the bench seat, having been properly warned by his mother of strangers who offered gifts. The old man smiled mysteriously at the wide-eyed boy at the end of the bench.

"No stomach for it, then, young sir? Well then, not to waste it. I'll just have it then."

With those words, the old man broke the light bulb between his teeth and made exaggerated eating sounds as he chewed the broken glass and swallowed it. The old man smiled, with shredded, bloody lips, at the boy.

The old man popped another light bulb in his mouth and young John ran screaming from the bench as if he himself had been attacked by the crazy old man.

He never looked back, never saw the old man again, but he saw the old man's bloodied mouth in his dreams for years after that.

Later, he had learned from his mother that the old man had escaped from a mental institution. He could never quite figure out why it was such a terrifying memory. Still in all, it was something that stayed with him all the years of his childhood. As an adult, he had pondered this puzzling memory from childhood and had satirically described it to himself in a very literary way. The old man represented the pitiful inadequacy of human illumination to combat the all-encompassing moral darkness of the world.

Other than this strange interlude, he had had a fairly idyllic childhood. He had been a toy in his own world of toys and had lived in a bright and all-too-shiny world for as long as he dared, much longer than all other children.

He wore fine suits of blue sateen with velveteen stripes all down the sides and fashioned into piping at every edge and seam. There were gilt epaulettes, buttons, braids, and a brave show of tiny medals and awards of mock valor, all painted gold and silver, stuck to his chest with fancy ribbons. He was dressed as a toy soldier and owned himself instead of having one.

There were miniature boots of red patent leather, a sword about as long as a broom straw, and a cockaded hat peaked front and back, which held a great, white, crested plume.

He had the costume made for him when he was five or six. He was the son and only child of a solicitor father and a gentlewoman mother. They were, as well, secretly ashamed of Colonel John, for they saw in his diminutive stature public evidence of their equally small passions. They did love him, however, in the same pale, unstressed, unheated way in which they loved each other.

They resided in an attached house of three stories in the favored quarter of London known as Kensington.

It was a special pleasure for young John to go for long walks with his mother through Kensington Gardens. He sailed little boats of his own making in the Serpentine. They explored the wonders of the bird sanctuary, oft times listened to concerts given at the bandstand close on to Park Lane and had tiffin from time to time in the Ring tea house. Twice, they even went so far as Marble Arch and stood with the colorful Sunday crowds listening to the public speakers on the Corner. But both times, his mother had had to carry him home, so weary had his little legs become. So, in consideration of that, such great walking journeys were curtailed.

When he was eight, John and his mother and father

went on a Sunday outing to the fun park at distant Batter-
sea. It was, by far, the farthest afield John had ever gone
from his home in Kensington.

As the three of them rested for a moment on long
wooden benches, a friendly woman in her middle years
tickled little John beneath the chin and remarked upon
what a splendid little fellow he was. When John thanked
her with careful and rather flowery courtesy, she was, at
first, much amused by the gay intelligence and eloquence
of such a young child. Then she peered closer and saw him
to be much older than the three years she had taken him
to be.

"Why, he's a midget!" cried the woman in surprise.

The father and mother exchanged a telling look over
John's head.

The woman hurried off to report the news of the child
midget to others of her acquaintance in the park. At last,
the not-so-casual glances of passersby—moving past with
deliberate intent, gathered to see this strange wonder,
this child freak—caused uncontrollable spasms in the
mother's hands and dark blotches of color above the collar
of the father's shirt.

They left in somewhat of a hurry and never entertained
the idea of such public display again.

From that moment, John's childhood became a private
and not a public one. And thus it was to be for quite some
time.

With the advent of war, however, there was forced a
need for moving out and about in the outside world. His
parents resisted the safety of the Underground shelters
for some time, stiff in their pride of person, but after the
great German air raid of September 7, 1940, and after
some long and almost tearful consultation together, his
parents decided they must use the crowded public bomb
shelters. A very near miss, just two doors away, had killed

two of their neighbors who also had not seen fit to take
shelter underground.

Young John's attention to the war was adult in quality.
He learned what he knew of it from the newspapers and
the B.B.C. Reading and listening to the wireless were
major parts of his occupation of the day, since he attended
no school and had been taught his lessons in grammar and
arithmetic by his mother and father. He had never been
registered for any school, and, indeed, as far as the proper
authorities were concerned, was not known to exist.

But he had visions of glory that were greater than those
of the adults around him—or perhaps merely more fantastic, since less practical. He fashioned dreams in which he
had miraculously grown tall—by now he had been taught
that this was something that life would deny him—and
fought as grown men fought.

His fairy-tale imaginings grew concrete and constant
when the first V-1, the "buzz bomb," fell upon London
some seven days after the invasion of the Continent.

Young John created a scenario that covered all practical
considerations. If the Germans had created such a
weapon, the British could make one as well. The newspapers declared that the V-1 bombs, though devastating in
their effect upon whatever structures they might hit,
were essentially a strategically useless weapon since they
could not be guided with accuracy to their targets.

And so, John went so far as to design an imaginary
missile, similar to pictures in the daily press of the flying
bombs caught in flight, that incorporated pilot's controls
and a tiny cockpit for someone as small as himself.

This machine of death, launched from a suitable site,
would, in his vivid imagination, fly to the very heart of
Berlin, to the Reichschancellory itself or, alternately, de-
pending on his dream, to the mountain fastness where the
evil genie, Adolf Hitler, sometimes dwelled. John would

fly his explosive little missile right through the window or
down through the chimney and kill the monster before he
could raise his arm and say "Heil Myself."

On a map of London, he traced the path he must take to
the Air Ministry in Whitehall where he intended to present his plan. There were great difficulties attending such
a journey since he had never, alone, ventured more than
one block from his house in any direction.

As the plan crystallized, the more terrible V-2 rockets
began to shower upon London. At last, his father decided
to send his small son out of danger.

John was delivered to his maiden aunt in Biddlestone, a
small village close to Bath in Wilts, who had neither ap-
proved of her brother's marriage or the birth of his unfor-
tunate son.

A week later, John's house and all it contained, includ-
ing his mother and father, were smashed down into a hole
in the ground. It became their final burial place. Very
little of them was found. John was, ashamedly, not particularly saddened by the news. It was not that he did not
love them—that, of course, he did—but rather it was that
he intuited that their deaths might well be the beginning
of his own life in the world so long denied him.

After the war, soon after his seventeenth birthday, he
ran away from his aunt—much to her relief—and Biddlestone, never to return. Like Dick Whittington, he went to
London—that strange and wonderful city of London that
he had never been allowed to know—in order to make his
fortune. He did not, of course, become Lord Mayor.

Instead, after a long and heartbreaking series of rebuffs
and cruel rejections, he found work in a discreet bordello
in Mayfair. It was, of course, not what he had expected or
sought. Still, it was the only place where the novelty of his
appearance added a certain glamour to the house of his
employment.

The madam of the house instructed him to dress in a velvet suit with a cavalier's ruff. It was an elegant house, patronized by the cream of British society—so the madam was at pains to explain to one and all. The madam considered herself a courtesan, not a prostitute, and very much acted out the role of a woman from the old Renaissance. John was a part of that delicate fabrication as well.

John endured, even enjoyed, the courtly pose and grand manner and began to think of himself as an actor.

Somewhat innocently, he enjoyed the company of the madam's young ladies, who took a delighted and affectionate comfort in his less fortunate presence. In time, nearly all of them took him companionably into their beds and taught him such wonders of touching and human closeness that made his grand dreams of noble, sacrificial death seem a damn foolishness beyond reasoning.

So skilled did he become, so gentle and so caring in his love play, that the time came when the young ladies of the house began somewhat jealously to fight over their affection for him. He became a disturbance and a liability to the peace of the house, and the madam did, at last and with much reluctance, let him go.

With great dreams—this time of being a great and noble actor the likes of Edmund Kean—John went to Soho, dressed like a miniature toff in green-checkered suits and yellow-gold shirts. His planned profession had no open doors for him, only a great deal of scorn and derision to heap on his small frame. Undaunted, John smoked big cigars and lived the part of the great actor he thought himself to be, living in grand style until the money ran out.

After the money was gone, John was forced to trade his dreams for less honorable things. Hunger brought new skills, albeit unhappy ones. He learned to pick pockets—which were eye level and amazingly handy to one of his

size—and roll drunks—not so handy—to supplement his
miniscule pay as a barker before the entrance of a girlie
show.

But always John dreamed of greater things. Variety
shows, night clubs, or even the cinema. He found his
chance when he was asked to join an English circus that
intended to invade and conquer the United States with "a
real, honest-to-Gawd English circus of the old fashioned
sort."

The year was 1955. Colonel John was twenty-five years
old.

The invasion was less than successful. The American
sponsor withdrew his support at the last moment. The
English impresario absconded with an incredibly ugly ele-
phant girl and a week's receipts, meager as they were.
John Featherstone, not yet a Colonel, not a war hero, not a
great actor, not a lot of things, was stranded in Philadelphia.

If there was a worse place to be stranded for a person
like John, he couldn't imagine where.

The Philadelphian winters of those years, as he worked
carnivals and store-front sideshows, were cold, too cold,
for his small bones. They reminded him of London and
made his heart want to return while his head insisted that
he remain and make his fortune.

His fortune was seven dollars and twenty-eight cents
when he took ill with a cold that settled in his chest. Three
of it went to the doctor who advised long bed-rest and
medicines beyond the competence of his purse.

He lay in the dark and chill of his mean room and
thought of his own death and was not surprised to find
that he desired it. Why not give over his life? Have an end
to the sorry view of garbage spinning through the gutters
of the city, finding his hat burned with the embers flicked

upon his head from cigarettes in the hands of passing strangers, the uncomfortable view that ladies afforded him, all unknowingly, of their garters. He was weary of chairs too wide to support his arms either side, too high to allow his feet to be placed upon the floor. Weary of bar stools that made him a figure of fun when he climbed them to order a man's drink. Tired of pointing fingers, whispers, and, perhaps worst of all, so everlastingly tired of the quickly turned heads of persons too polite to stare.

He folded his hands upon his chest and upon the sheet that covered him. He closed his eyes. The dark of this mean room was that of the grave. It was peaceful.

He was irked when the knock sounded tentatively upon the door. He was in the third day of his death, having gone without food and spending the time spiritually preparing himself for the end. The tapping, like a frightened mouse, sounded again, and John, somewhat testily, shouted that whoever it was who meant to desecrate his final resting time should come in. He supposed it to be the landlady on the subject of the rent.

He opened his eyes and regarded the pale girl who stood uncertainly within his doorway upon the worn carpet.

"I hadn't seen you about for several days. . . ." she began.

"Several? Has it been several?" John asked cheerfully.

"Three at least."

His smile left him. "I had hoped it was more. You said several."

"Well, several is more than two. It can be three."

"Three is a few, not several. Sit down and tell me what you want."

She sat down beside him, her eyes anguished, lips dry and fingers making patterns upon themselves.

"I don't want anything. I just hadn't seen you about and

thought . . . thought perhaps you were ill," she said somewhat shyly.

"I am. I am dying," said John. "Although that is not so much a disease as the cure for one."

She gasped, quite startled by the news.

"Of what . . . But I didn't even know. . . ." She was quite confused. "It must be very sudden. I hadn't even known you were sick."

"No. Not sudden. More's the pity. It seems damnably slow. I am starving to death and a preciously tedious way to go, too, I might add."

She gave a gasp and he reached out a hand to comfort her.

She looked very unhappy for him.

"There, there, my dear, it shouldn't concern you. I feel little enough pain. I have a cold with the attendant benumbing ache and my senses are so befuddled I suffer very little."

"But it seems so unfair."

Colonel John nodded his head. "Ah, yes. I can only agree. But still, your visit in this last act of my life is a pleasant surprise."

"But must you die?"

"I've had little choice. I am without funds, without food, and without hope."

"And if those things were offered to you, what would you say?"

A tear formed in the corner of one of his eyes.

"But we are strangers, but briefly met in the lobby and you know nothing of me."

"Every friend I've ever met was a stranger until I met him," she said, and smiled softly at him.

Colonel John felt a warm pang flow through his cold body, as if a ray of sunlight had shown through the window, warming him with its heat.

"You are wonderfully kind. But I fear it is too late. I'm so cold I must be dead or nearly so."

"I have some very nourishing hot soup in my room."

"Hot soup?"

"I know it's not allowed, but I have a little hot plate on which to cook my meals."

"So do I and so does nearly everyone in this tenement of bad fortune."

She blushed as though she thought he was somehow scolding her.

"Shall I get it?"

Colonel John flushed with embarrassment. "I am not sure I can repay your suggested kindness."

"I don't expect you to. I'll just dash off and get it." With that she got up and left the room.

When she was gone to fetch the soup, John thought to rise from his bed, the better to receive his guest but he was almost unable to move his head, let alone rise. He had hoped to don his red-velvet smoking jacket and at least wash his face and comb his hair, but it would have to wait. The idea of being tended and fussed over appealed to him. Flickeringly, he thought of the way his mother, so long ago, had fussed over him when he was ill as a child. It was the warmest love he'd ever received from her.

The girl's name was Susy and she worked as a clerk in a five-and-dime, whose prices had long ago ceased being five and ten cents.

She came back into the room and propped his head up on the pillow and fed him the warm soup, with apparent pleasure in the task. It was somewhat akin to nursing a tiny bird with a broken wing until it was strong enough to fly again.

When she had spooned the thick, creamy broth down him, he shivered and still complained of being cold. Her eyes darted about, seeking other blankets with which to cover him, but the barren room held no more.

He touched her hand with his own well-formed one. "Are you cold, as well?" There was no guile in his voice.

"I have been cold all my life," she said in a voice of sadness.

"Ah," he said, nodding companionably. "Then we have shared much of the same long, cold night."

She pondered his tiny, shivering body for a time and then, finally, drew the coverlet aside and, still dressed, crawled in beside him. Her body, touching his, didn't start at the contact. She was not repelled. Perhaps she felt safe with him. A small lover—for that's what they were soon to be to each other—that would not hurt her or be unfaithful to her dreams.

And so they fell in love and moved, after John's recovery, south to escape the cold winters. It was an uneasy love affair. They sometimes spoke of marriage but never quite came round to it. They found themselves somehow unable to find one particular place that suited them. The longer they stayed in a place, the less it seemed to suit them. Just why this was, neither could say.

After a few years of wandering, they found themselves at last in Charleston, Kanewha County, West Virginia, and it was there that Susy and John fell out of love once and for all.

John tried to still her fears, to reassure her, but, the battle once entered upon, could not be stilled until the war was won or lost.

She became shrewish because she had to find things on which to blame John—failures, real and imagined, on which she could pillory him, the better to exorcise the real demon, the underlying truth she could not quite admit to herself.

Her voice became thin and querulous, raised in a continual litany of scorn and abuse.

Slowly, John's awareness of her changed. She was, he finally realized, a most unattractive creature. Her hair had the consistency and color of shredded wheat. Her eyes, while not actually crossed, were so close together as to make her appear forever looking at the tip of her nose. As her mouth moved, spilling out her frustrations of the time past, he saw her lips as shapeless bits of pure petulance, and wondered to himself that they had once tasted sweet to him. But yet, he did love her.

"Why here?" he asked. "Why have you reached the breaking point in Charleston, of all places?"

She just glared at him, thinking him stupid, thinking the question stupid, too.

"Why the hell not? I'm sick and tired of filthy hotel rooms and rooming houses and washing my underwear out in the sink!" said Susy.

"As if it were my fault alone. You said we should move on at least as often as I did, perhaps even more times than I did. It's you that . . ." began John reasonably.

"Don't hand me that line of guff. I've had it with you. I'm fed up with lousy food in crummy restaurants."

John stared at her in surprise. "Through good times and bad, at least we've had each other."

"There have been no good *times.* Only stinking, miserable ones, a day late and a dollar short."

"Come now, my love," he began but she would have none of it. She ranted on at him at great length.

At last, John began to see what was really bothering her. Not the places they had been, the economic situation in which they were trapped. It was being with him, having to cope with his condition, having to face the rest of the world coupled with what seemed only half of a man.

How much it must pain her, thought John, how cruel

and unkindly the world out there must treat her, certainly much worse than they treat me. I have no choice in the matter but she is with me by choice and surely the world heaps scorn on her for what must be in their minds a very bad choice.

He smiled rather wistfully. "Have you so hated being with me all these years. Have I been that unkind, that unloving to you?"

She turned her back on him.

"No." It was, at best, a grudging admission.

He looked at the body that had warmed him, that had once brought him back to life, and gave her a compliment. "Since we first met, in your way, your body has grown more womanly, all the more lovely, while mine has stayed its small self, not an inch taller."

She ignored the compliment, remaining silent.

"What is it you want?" he asked.

"To settle down somewhere. Anywhere."

It was not what she wanted, not what she wanted of him, but it was as good an excuse to combat as any other she could devise.

"I'll see what can be done," promised John. "Tomorrow."

"No you bloody well won't." She whirled back to face him. "You'll go out right now and see to steady work this morning or I'll . . ." The threat trembled in the air.

Good Lord, thought John, she is playing a part from a really bad motion picture. Was she being Bette Davis? There was no grace or lasting truth to the scene and John grew angry with offense. How had it come that he should have become burdened with such an impossible creature, and she with him, a pairing as doomed as any that ever met.

He supposed she really did love him. And no doubt

hated herself for placing her love in so small and unsuitable a vessel.

"Then let us not go on in this manner. The fact is, my life has always been," he said—joining her in the same bad movie, of spurious lines and mock heroics—"devoted to the life of the open road. I am a loner by nature, a free spirit. Almost a minstrel, as it were, a wandering player, needing ever to travel on."

"Liar. You're just a little man! A child really!" she said with calculated cruelty.

"I am a young giant," he said, wanting somehow to make light of the situation.

"You are a forty-one-year-old midget."

"A lady does not confront a gentleman with the indelicate matter of his age." The fine high mockery in his tone!

She shook her head in disbelief. The pomposity of the little man enraged her.

He went to the door, holding it carefully so that he might slam it with a satisfactory bang when he went through it. "We will have to discuss this whole affair later when we can both be civilized about it. Perhaps two years from now."

"What the hell are you talking about?"

He opened the door.

"Where the hell do you think you are going?" she yelled at him, arms akimbo.

"To ride a bomb into Adolf Hitler's lap," he said, and the door slammed most pleasingly and finally as he left.

Instead, John took a beer in the corner tavern and stared out the window, feeling terribly alone and lost when he saw her hurry by the window, dressed in her best dress and wearing her highest and most ridiculous heels.

For no reason he could explain, John followed her.

She stopped at a movie theater, whose marquee announced that it was inaugurating a policy of vaudeville with their cinema offerings, in a nostalgic—and they vainly hoped profitable—salute to yesteryear. John bought a ticket and followed Susy into the darkened theater. A number of variety turns were in progress as John took a seat at some distance behind her.

There was on the program an act billed as "Will Carney, Juggler Extraordinaire." It was an all too familiar act, but John noted that Susy leaned forward in her seat as though enchanted by the performer's admittedly graceful hands. At the conclusion of the olio, Susy left her seat and walked to the front, where the juggler was making his bows to a not very impressed audience. The juggler caught her eye and her eager look. He bowed deeply to her and said several phrases under his breath, loud enough only for her to hear. She smiled with pleasure, a look John noted, as she turned from the stage and began walking back up the aisle.

The juggler was replaced by a dance team that had seen

better and younger days. The two old parties whirled
across the stage with arthritic abandon.

As Susy walked past John's seat he wanted to speak out
to her, but, instead, he lowered his head until he appeared
to be a man bending over in search of something in the
dark and so went unnoticed.

Cursing himself for a fool, John sat slumped in his theater seat. Changing his mind yet again, he bolted up from
the seat and hurried to catch up to her. He made it out the
front just in time to see her go into a coffee shop just across
the street.

John stood on the sidewalk, trying to make up his mind.
Did he want to see her? Should he let her go her own way
as he must go his? And if he did catch up to her, was it
worth making a scene in public, as no doubt Susy would
insist in doing? John suddenly felt very weary. He turned
away then, retracing his steps, considering returning to
their cheap rented room. I must call my booking agent
and discover why I was not called upon to audition for the
theater owner who was offering vaudeville, John thought.
As he walked, out of the corner of his eye, he saw the
juggler, Will Carney, sweeping past on the other side of
the street with a determined walk.

Something in the juggler's manner caused John to
pause and turn back again to look at the café. Through the
clear glass windows, he saw the small pantomime of Susy's
and the juggler's meeting, the too bright smiles to cover
shyness. John was ashamed at the simpering way Susy
seemed to hang on the juggler's every phrase.

Well, I simply don't give a damn, thought John. I won't
be trifled with. I won't allow myself to be the third man in
a triangle so commonplace. I won't be provoked. And yet
he found himself hiding in the shadow of a billboard,
pretending he did not care, but unable to look away, sens-

ing as he watched them—Susy and the juggler—a new
and terrible change in his life.

Susy and the juggler left the coffee shop together, arm
in arm, soon after, and John—very much ashamed of not
being strong enough not to—followed them to a rooming
house no less dark and cold than his own. John stood out in
the street and looked up at the dark windows until a light
was turned on up on the third floor. A man's hand reached
out and pulled down a stained and weathered window
shade. John imagined that the shadow of a woman—Susy,
of course—came into an embrace with the shadow of the
juggler. It all belonged to Susy's bad movie.

John began to laugh. It was not a happy laugh, steeped
as it was in dark irony. It all seemed so tawdry and predict-
able. Why should he, a man who, while still a boy, had
volunteered to fly a suicide mission to Germany and destroy Hitler, be forced to take a part in this ridiculous
charade.

So John straightened his shoulders and marched off
down the street, vowing not to return, but he didn't get
very far. He spent a frustrating half hour pacing up and
down the street until a cop gave him a warning when
John, in inexplicable fury, had kicked over a couple of
garbage cans. John found himself again outside the rooming house in which Susy and the juggler were making a
damned fool out of him.

The bloody, flaming hell with it, swore John and, swag-
gering in an unconscious imitation of Bogart, he stormed
his way up several flights of stairs—several *can* be three
but there were six—until he reached the proper door. I
suppose I should have a gun or a baseball bat or some
other instrument of violence, he thought to himself as he
made a small fist and hammered on the door. He tilted his
hat on his head till it had a tough-guy tilt, movie-style.

There were muffled sounds of irritation from the room

within, the creaking of bedsprings, and the squeak of ancient floors before he heard the voice of the juggler ask who it was and what was wanted.

"Telegram," John said, knowing that entertainers always hoped for and expected one.

John had both his hands balled into fists, ready to do battle, however ineffectual and one-sided it might be.

The door opened a crack and John pushed his way into the room with sudden strength. Susy, wide-eyed, clutched the sheet to her bosom and ducked down in the bed as if looking for a place to hide. The juggler stood at the door, holding his trousers on with one hand, and scratching his head in pure bewilderment with the other.

John struck a fighting pose in front of the astonished juggler. The juggler let loose an involuntary exclamation of surprise. John, taking it as a cue, swung on him then and there, the blow glancing ineffectually off the juggler's bony hip. But the juggler ruined it all. He began to laugh, not in a small way, but in a big, uproarious guffaw that filled the entire room.

John had his fists poised to strike again, dancing on the balls of his feet, but found himself unable to hit a man convulsed with laughter.

"Well, I'll be rolled up and bounced like a ball," cried the juggler, his voice registering great delight. "I'll be plain, downright fried and tied if this don't beat all. I say, my good man, who the dickens are you?"

It was as if John had never struck him at all.

"I am," said John, dropping the fists he now realized he wasn't going to use, "that woman's husband."

"You're not! You're not!" Susy protested, almost dropping the sheet and exposing herself.

"I'll be pruned and piano tuned," said Will Carney, staring at the little man with unmistakable curiosity. "Don't that beat anything."

"Well, common-law married, at any rate," John ammended.

"Holy Kee-rist on skates! I can't believe this," the juggler said, and self-consciously zipped up his fly. "If this isn't the ever-loving end, I don't know what is."

Susy, sensing a fight, jumped out of bed. The sheet slipped out of her hands and fell away.

"You cover yourself, woman. Don't you have no shame, woman?" said the juggler, as if assuring John of his own decency.

Susy sniffed disapprovingly and turned her back on them. She cursed under her breath as she eased back into her rumpled clothes.

The juggler ignored her and, with a little formal bow, asked John if he would take a chair. Caught by surprise, by the juggler's politeness and manners, John numbly shook his head yes, for he was quite at a loss for something to do. This wasn't going quite as he had hoped it would.

"It's a pleasure to meet you, sir. You are really quite something. As small and just about as perfect as any I've ever seen or ever will see."

"You haven't seen much then," John said, bristling and preening at the compliment all in the same moment.

"Not all there is to see, I grant you. But, my good man, I've seen plenty, far and wide, and I tell you right to your face, you are a proper wonder."

Susy glared angrily at the two of them, as John felt his face flush with pleasure.

"And that entrance! Why, no actor in the history of theater has done quite as good a comic turn as that!" raved the juggler, choosing to misinterpret the act. "I swear I don't know when I ever laughed so!"

The juggler practically gushed with praise for the little man. In the voice of a rather stupid Southern hick, the juggler went on. "Well, I declare. I haven't had so much fun since the hogs up and ate my brother."

John laughed in spite of himself. The juggler surely was a master at putting a fellow to ease.

Susy was only the more enraged.

"Are you in the business?" asked the juggler.

"I am an actor, yes," said John with pride.

"Do I know the name?" asked the juggler.

"What are you talking to that miserable little creep for?" said Susy, all too aware of their indifference to her. They didn't act as if they had heard a single word she had said.

"My name is John Feather. Actually, Featherstone."

"Why, sure. Why, hell yes, I've heard of you," lied the juggler. "You're all but damn-well famous, you are."

John cleared his throat, basking in a sudden glow, readying a modest demurrer.

"But badly mismanaged, I'd say. Isn't that the truth?" asked the juggler.

"Well . . . yes, it is," John allowed, warming to the crisp friendliness and levelheadedness of the juggler. John could not but help like his open grin, could not help admiring the way he gestured with his slender, clever hands.

"You're damn right. I call them as I see them," the juggler said. "My name's Will Carney, by the by." He stuck out his hand with such a spirit of hail-fellow that John took it and was glad of the chance.

"Would you like a beer?"

"I would love one."

"How about you, honey?" There was a hesitation after "you" and before "honey" that said clearly that Will Carney had already forgotten Susy's name.

"No. I don't want nothing," she said in a voice choked with rage.

John winced at her poor grammar as he would were she an illiterate child of his own. Will opened a pair of beers and handed one over to John.

"Now, see, that's what I always did say."

"What?"

"I always said, no agent, no ten percenter is going to do the proper job for the artist. No sir. Got to do it for yourself or . . ." He took a long pull on the beer and licked his lips.

"Yes?" John said, leaning forward with an eagerness and hope he'd not experienced for a long time.

"Or have somebody close do it for you. Better yet, artists get together and do it for each other."

"Do what?"

"Bring what they got to the public attention."

Susy tapped her foot impatiently against the floor. She cleared her throat loudly several times to get their attention but they paid her no heed.

"Will Carney, aren't you going to throw this little weasel out?" she said.

The juggler looked at her as if she had suddenly started speaking Swahili or some other foreign tongue. "Now why ever would I want to do that?"

"Well, he broke right in here while we was . . ." She left it unsaid; the telling apparently was more immoral than the doing.

"Well, it's clear to me this fellow came up here to protect his woman. No idea what would be waiting for him. Some mean bastard, maybe, who would do him harm for butting in. Why, you seldom find a 'true artiste' would take the risk of hurting himself. He's brave, truly brave."

"You better damn well throw him out on his ear if you want me to stay around," said Susy, looking mean.

The juggler winked conspiratorily at John, who grinned

in pleasure. "Well, if you're too far away to touch, you'll be too far away to see, won't you?"

She stood there looking from Will's white grin to John's sad eyes. She trembled all over and then turned away. When she was at the door, John wanted to run and stop her. He wanted to take her back home and call her his own, but Will started talking, about the open road, about the carefree life of the traveling 'artiste,' and suddenly there were bright visions dancing before John's eyes and he settled back in his chair, Susy forgotten. He closed his eyes the better to be entranced by the smooth river of promises that tumbled from Will Carney's mouth.

And so, having dawdled with his woman—who was never seen or heard of again—Will Carney contracted John Feather—without contract or signature—to join his company, made him a Colonel, and changed his name.

On the very top of that particular face of the mountain, the seams of rotting stone shale were sucking up the rain, swelling just that little bit, loosening up just that fraction. Capillary action drew it deep under the cap of the hill and gorged the rootlets of the clinging moss till they burst and broke apart. A whole shelf of shale slipped, two hundred feet above the truck, dropping a few feet, hinging on something, threatening at any moment to continue its plunge and wipe the truck and its occupants off the side of the mountain once and for all time. The whole mountain shuddered to its heart.

It was about to lose a piece of itself and it knew it, as did the occupants of the truck, who could feel the heaving shale shifting under them almost as if it were an animal turning over in its sleep under them in the darkness.

It was getting hot as hell inside the van. Inside the cab as
well. Strangely, it seemed to affect Marco the most. The
bleeding had slowed but by no means stopped. His face
was pale, wracked with pain. He tapped Will's arm and
made a motion, telling him in pantomime to roll down his
window. The one on his side was blocked with dirt a
quarter of the way up and he had no need or desire for a
ton of it in his lap. Will opened the window and found the
angle of the cab had slipped so that the rain, even blowing
around as it was, didn't enter the space. The truck was ten
degrees off center, canting over toward the chasm side.

There was no window to roll down in the van though
some bit of relief came from the cab through the broken
communication pane. The Colonel felt a bit of it cool the
skin of his face. He lifted his hands to catch the breeze
upon his forearms. He quickly occupied himself in remov-
ing his shirt. He stooped to the tangle of ropes that bound
Serena to the floor. His hands were trembling. The sight
of this weakness set him to trembling all over. He dis-
guised his panic in action.

There was blood on one of Serena's white stockings.

"You're hurt, my little lady love," he murmured.

"I scarcely feel it. My legs are nearly numb." In truth,
she was in great pain, but not from her injuries. It was
Marco's pain that troubled her most. It was like a fire that
burned in her own body, so greatly did she sense it, did

she share it with the gentle giant in the front compartment.

Her own shoulder throbbed as if it too felt the bone-shattering impact of the bullet. It burned, it ached. It raged against her outraged nerve endings as if someone had placed a red-hot coal against her delicate white body.

Colonel John bent over her solicitiously. "I'll have your dear little legs out from under the ropes and tent rigging quick as a wink. Not to worry. Just be patient, my little darling."

"I will, Colonel John. I will." She trusted him implicitly.

He grasped hold of a coil of rope. His child-hands wouldn't quite circle it. When he heaved on the little he could manage to grasp, the ropes and tent poles massed in a resisting clump, intertwining like the rings of a magician's trick. If he went on, he'd only create a greater tangle of it all.

He took off his belt and passed it round a coil of the rope, fitting the tongue through the buckle and drawing it tight. He sought purchase for his feet on the floor and put his weight to the belt as though playing at tug-of-war. The leather heels of his fashionable boots slipped on the sweating steel and he fell painfully upon his hip. He turned the other way about, and passing the belt over his shoulder, he hauled forward like a tiny pony in its traces. He made some small progress and then Serena suddenly cried out in great pain.

The tangled ropes came free all at once and the Colonel stumbled forward in a rush, tent poles and riggings tumbling after him like an odd-looking tumbleweed.

Colonel John was up on his feet in an instant and back at Serena's side as quick as he could move. He was at once on his knees beside her. "What is it? How have I hurt you?"

Her small teeth had caught her lip between them. As she sighed with the passing of the sharpness of that first outcry, it was released. A tiny droplet of ruby blood welled and glistened there until her tongue brushed it away.

"Oh. Oh. Oh," she said. Her lovely hands made patterns in the air above her stockinged legs, wanting to touch herself but afraid to do so.

The Colonel looked at her poor, atrophied limbs again. Cleared of most of the obscuring rope, he could see far more blood than was, at first, evident.

"My brave little one," he nearly cried. He felt her large, shapely hand fall feather-soft upon his head. It was like being touched by an angel. Their voices were so soft as to be the murmurings of lovers. "I'm afraid to move it anymore."

She gasped. "Is it broken?"

"I'm not a doctor. What do I know of such things?"

He was worried, frightened. He felt his confidence slipping, his command of the situation eluding him. Serena sense it in him and would not allow him that.

She said, with the utmost calm and assurance in her voice, "Dear John, you are very wise. Your eyes are sharp. I think you know."

Colonel John regained himself, becoming almost fatherly in his ministrations.

"My love, it's not so bad. Not so very bad at all. If you could only see, you'd know I was telling the truth." John hoped with all his heart that what he said was true, for he was only guessing.

"I will see it," she said.

Her hand, the sensitive fingers scarcely seeming to touch, appraised the damage to that most useless part of her body—she did not conceive of her blindness as her greatest handicap—and Serena even managed a smile.

"You are quite masterful, my dear Colonel. And right, in that it is not so very bad. But it is very painful. I don't think

I could bear to have it jostled about any more." The pain was not all that unbearable but it distracted her. Too much of it would rob her of her power and she felt she must save as much of herself for the task before her. The long nightmare of the night was only beginning.

"What are you whispering about?" Will's voice suddenly demanded, fear large in his manner. "Are you figuring out ways to save yourselves and to leave me here to die?"

"Serena's leg has been injured, almost broken, Will," the Colonel said in a natural voice. He seemed calmer. In a way the raw, naked fear in Will's voice seemed to steady him. At least he had better control of himself than Will had.

"Don't whisper about it, if that's what it really is," complained Will. "I want to know what the hell you're up to back there?"

"Mind your business, Will," said Colonel John.

"Mind my business? Mind my business? Everything you do is my damn business. You work for me, remember? You belong to me?"

The Colonel cut him off with a laugh. "No more." It struck him suddenly as being funny. He almost giggled. "We don't work for you now, Will, and we never did belong to you."

As he said it, Colonel John understood it to be true. It had always been true but until that moment, until he had just spoken it for himself and for all of them, he had not really known it. The knowledge of it made him feel even more powerful.

It affected the others, too. Paulette started to giggle and Pepino began to roar with laughter. Serena, even in pain, laughed a little, too.

"Are you crazy? What the hell are you all laughing

about?" Will screamed at them. "Are you all going crazy back there?"

The Colonel had a big grin on his face when he sang out, "We'd all appreciate it, Will, if you would kindly shut your big, fat mouth."

"Who the hell do you think you're talking to?" raged Will Carney. He twisted violently in his seat, like an animal finding itself suddenly cornered.

Marco regarded Will Carney curiously. In the dimness of the cab's interior he noted Will's wild eyes like those of crazed, unbroken horses. He saw flecks of spittle in the corners of Will's mouth. He could not hear the words shouted in the dark but he understood the sense of them, the torment and the anxiety. He felt it himself.

Only the Strong Man's splendid physique and marvelously rugged constitution kept him conscious. The pain was almost too much to bear, yet he was awake, conscious of all that transpired around him. Will worried him as much as anything. He feared Will would do something stupid.

"I own this carnival. I own this truck. I own you. All of you. Where the hell would you all be without me?" cried Will.

The Colonel's voice came liltingly into the cab. "One place we wouldn't be, Will. We wouldn't be clinging to the side of this rain-swept mountain, in a night as black as a black bear's lap. We wouldn't be where we are, that's for sure, just a few seconds away from death."

"Blame it on me, you bastard. Now you listen to what I have to tell you," Will raged. He was trying to turn around in his seat. The truck began to wobble as his movements disturbed the delicate equilibrium.

Marco saw that Will was completely losing control. His uninjured arm came up and his heavy hand shot across the space between them and slapped Will across the mouth.

Will was stunned by the force of the blow. He gasped like a drowning man, and slid back into place behind the wheel. He held his face with his hands and started to cry softly.

Everyone was quiet of a sudden, listening with deep embarrassment to his cowardly sobbing. They were at once humiliated and fearful, for they had, indeed, once made Will Carney master of their lives. Now, that master was too weak and useless to help them in their time of need.

Now, they had only themselves and a dream. Only a dream between them and death.

Paulette, Serena, and Pepino turned their eyes upon the Colonel. He met their stare unflinchingly. He sensed their meaning, felt their unspoken trust.

He spoke with more authority than he felt. "First, I'll bind up your leg, sweet Serena, as gently as I can."

He tore his shirt into ribbons and used them as bandages. His small hands were as delicate as a bird's touch as he wound the cloth about the girl's injured leg. Her unseeing, luminous eyes seemed to be staring lovingly into his very heart as she withstood the agony his ministrations caused her. When he was done, she sighed. She touched his shoulder.

"Truly you are a giant," she said as her gift of thanks. "You have a most perfect body, like a miniature *David* by Michelangelo."

He knew it wasn't so, but he thanked her with sweet shyness.

"I may have to hurt you still more," he said.

She simply nodded.

"Most of the riggings and rope bundles are off you now.

I'm going to lift off the rest. Can you slide yourself out from underneath when I ask you to?"

"I will try."

It was the strength in her saying that, that gave Colonel John his strength back. He seized hold of the ropes and with muscles straining, heaved the weight off her. Serena placed her hands upon the floor and at his gasped "now," dragged herself free along a river of pain.

The Colonel emitted a strangled cry of success and let fall his burden. They rested.

"There's so much more to be done," the Colonel said after a while.

"Just tell us what to do. We're with you, Colonel John." Pepino said it for them all.

Serena was moved, with the Colonel's care and her own strong arms, to a place beside the separation of van and cab. The Colonel instructed her to place her hands upon the metal wall.

"Now's the time and place for you to make use of your beautiful hands, Serena. You must read the shifting of the truck as you read the words on a page."

"I will, John. Trust me on that." She smiled to show that she was not afraid. In truth, terror was lurking just behind her smile. She feared that the pain in her legs had rendered her powerless, had removed her as a force to move them all. But she smiled bravely enough for their sakes.

Colonel John, cautiously and with infinite stealth, moved a pair of cartons and piled them one atop the other beneath the communicating window. He climbed them and put head and shoulders through the window into the cab. There were tears in his eyes as he surveyed, for the first time, the bloody ruin that had been visited upon Marco. Oh Christ! He recoiled, almost plunging back through the window, but somehow, from some place in a dream inside himself, he found the courage to grin at Marco, who smiled softly in return.

"I'm afraid you're done for, Marco," whispered Colonel John, mouthing the words so Marco could read them. The others could not hear the midget. "It looks to be a grievous wound."

Marco nodded. He shrugged. He understood there was nothing to be done about it. Only Serena knew him to be wrong.

Colonel John looked then to Will Carney whose body was still racked by sobs from time to time.

"I'm coming through. I will climb out the window and then onto the roof," said Colonel John, his eyes bright with tears for Marco, for them all.

Despite his grief, there was steel in his voice, a determination that spoke for all of them. He said it as Alexander must have spoken when he announced his determination to conquer Darius.

Paulette watched his tiny feet leave their place upon the boxes as the Colonel heaved himself up.

Upon the mountain, the shelf of shale slipped a full yard. The mountain seemed to cry out. The shock wave ran through its bones. Some metal part in the body of the van sang out, vibrating like an insect. There was the merest trembling in the body of the truck. It was transferred to the interior panel, which Serena touched.

"Stop!" she said, in a voice that froze Colonel John in place.

The Colonel hung in space, looking like a child seeking cookies from the high pantry shelf.

"The truck is trembling," said Serena.

She kept her magic hands in place during the seemingly interminable time it took for the midget to make his way back down on the boxes. He hesitated there, then stepped back cautiously to the floor. Serena's hands read the tremors and vibrations. She knew it was the mountain itself that had shuddered. It was that force that had moved the truck, not that the Colonel had overbalanced it. It was a difficult thing to sense in the dark and she strained for the right answer, the right choice.

Serena's hands touched a tremor that was death for them all.

The rain fell undiminished.

The Colonel examined the intricacies of the Chinese puzzle of gear and goods that kept Pepino imprisoned. The right arm and head of the Rubber Man were free but his movement was otherwise severely limited.

"Move your right arm," the Colonel said.

As Pepino moved it cautiously, defining the parameters of motion, the midget watched most carefully.

"Now the left leg."

Pepino drew it up by trying to set it free of a small maze of aluminum tent rods. They fell with a clatter and a ringing that seemed to go on for a long time.

"Do you need me again?" Serena asked from the gloom.

"We do," said the Colonel.

He moved Serena in his strong arms with the tenderest of care to the place closest to Pepino's left leg. As Serena touched first this and then some other thing, the Colonel removed a rod here, a box or bag there. Her hands, like

tossed it into the van through the broken window. It nearly struck the Colonel, smashing at the Midget's feet.

The Midget cried, "Oh Christ! Are you drunk? Are you both drunk?"

"Nobody's drunk, you goddamn half-pint," Will shouted. He started to laugh. "Damn it, if you only was a half pint of mountain dew, how I would hug and kiss and love yew, yew, yew." He belched.

"You'd better settle down in there, Will," threatened the Colonel. "You'll do for us all if you don't."

"You settle down, you little whey-faced weasel! What the hell should we settle down for! We'll be settled all right! Settled underneath the mud at the bottom of this gorge. Might as well flip us over the edge and have done with it." Will started to claw at the handle of the door. "I'm going to step out for a breath of fresh air. Too hot in here," he said loudly.

Will slammed his shoulder against the door. The truck heaved and canted over. The van was filled with screams. Marco grappled with Will and dragged him in one quick wrenching jerk back into the cab. He held Will close to his chest as though they were lovers. With just the one useful arm, he wrapped Will up and applied pressure slowly, tightening like a human boa constrictor against Will's chest. The air was driven from Will's lungs. He thrashed about and tried to strike the Strong Man but Marco held him so tightly that he scarcely moved an inch. Will's vision grew dark. Marco was unrelenting. Will passed out.

Marco released him and arranged his unconscious body so that Will's head lay upon the cushion of the seat next to him. Serena, in the back, despite her great weariness, was the only one in the van aware of the silent Strong Man's struggle. She had been in his mind, seeing and feeling Will's interference. She had felt Marco's quiet disapproval of the man's drunken behavior. Marco's strength was deeply engrained not just in his body but in his mind, as well. Tasting his strength made her a little stronger.

Marco, perhaps made more aware by his own imminent death, was aware of the presence of Serena in his mind. He did not seem surprised. He was in too much pain to do more than sort of dully be aware of her, of the strange power the tiny Moon Child revealed to him.

Serena gasped, jerking spasmodically. The pain from Marco was overpowering now, wracking her own tiny, frail body.

Marco touched his own chest and a spasm of great pain passed across his eyes like the shadow of a raven's wing. Glistening drops of sweat like quicksilver sprang out on his forehead. His face was the color of old linen.

A lesser man would have been dead long ago.

And there was a great part of him that wanted to sleep in that terrible and final way. But Serena was there and dreamed otherwise.

Soon, I shall let you go. Soon, promised Serena. Hold on, my sweet, whispered Serena in his mind. Stay just a little longer. We need you.

Marco smiled to himself; he agreed with her, forcing himself to stay awake just a little bit longer, but he was afraid it was a promise he could not long keep.

The Midget did not understand the silence from the front, not completely, but Serena was there to reassure him ever so gently, probing his fears and doubts and easing them with the touch of her gentle hands. In any case, there was much that had to be done. The Colonel reckoned that Marco had probably done something to Will to quiet him. Still, Will's behavior had sent renewed panic coursing through him.

He turned hurriedly to appraising the welter of material that clogged the escape hatch of the van.

"Can you try again, my Serena? Have you the strength

to go on?" he asked gently. "Can you listen with your
hands and your fingertips once more to the boxes and
bales?"

"Yes." Her answer reassured him in the gloom of the
truck.

"I'll have to move you to the wall of things. Pepino's
free now. The two of us shall carry you between us."

They made a cat's cradle of their arms, Pepino remaining on his knees to even off the height of them. Serena
swung her legs off the floor by the strength of her long,
white arms and settled herself into their embrace. They
took her to the face of all the poles, ropes, trunks, cases,
boxes, bales, cartons, kitchenware, clothing, towels, canvas, and all and all.

Serena touched the tangle and confusion of it, tested
first one item, then another, hauling on the one while
touching the other to sense it's trembling and, therefore,
it's balance.

"It's a house of cards," Serena said at last. "If any one
thing is pulled out from anywhere . . ."

"Even from the top?" the Colonel interrupted.

"From anywhere, anywhere. The whole thing might
come tumbling down."

They placed her on the floor close to Paulette's feet.
Paulette petted Serena's hair.

"We'll rest some, and look and touch again," the Colonel said.

Pepino threw his back to rest the muscles of his neck.
His attenuated sinews and tendons were not worthy of
extended effort.

"Look there," he suddenly said.

The Colonel looked where Pepino regarded the ceiling
of the van. He looked at the ventilator.

"Can you reach it?" the Midget asked.

"I can try."

Pepino moved cautiously to a point just beneath the small hatch. The ventilator was of the type that contained vanes such as those upon the roofs of houses. They spin with the breezes and draw fresh and cooling air into the attic space beneath the eaves. In such a way the ventilator of the van was set in motion when the truck drove along, sucking in cooling drafts.

Pepino raised his hands far above his head but still the crown was higher. He worked his trick loosening the joints at hip, shoulder, elbow, and wrist until he had grown, his arms had grown, and his fingertips touched the ring that held the housing in place. His fingers grasped the seam and tried to work their tips in so far as to create a wedge of flesh beneath the roof. He clawed. Bits of paint fell into his upturned face but he could not budge the retainer. He released his hold and lowered his arms. The joints and muscles sang with pain.

"I need something to pry under the lip of the retainer. A screwdriver."

"The pry bar?"

"Too thick, I think."

The Midget went stealthily along to the pry bar which Serena had dropped upon the floor when its purpose was done. It was too thick for this job, as Pepino had said.

"Will! Will!" he called. "There's a screwdriver in the glove compartment. Give it to me. Will? Will?"

Will was unconscious still and Marco could not hear. He lay with his huge back canted to the window, his cheek against it, grateful for the slight coolness it gave. His chest was held in a great vise. There was the tiniest of poppings in his ears, tiny movements of his system.

I am ready to die now. He thought this as much for Serena's sake as his own. He started, aware of a strange strength born suddenly within him, a strength that was

not his alone. The pain was unbearable, the urge for the
final sleep almost irresistible.

Serena was bathed in sweat, her body shaking with the
effort she now expended. She was everywhere in Marco's
huge body. She was the beating of his heart and the shal-
low hiss of air flowing into his laboring lungs.

Just a little longer, brave Marco.

Marco opened his eyes, staring into the emptiness of the
night.

His lips formed a silent plea, understanding at last the
struggle within himself that was not his fight alone.

No, Serena, let me go. He thought a silent plea at her.

But her dream was as strong as the force of life itself and
she would not surrender, even in the face of his great
pain.

Marco closed his eyes.

It was too hard to fight both death and a dream.

For him there was no release.

It wasn't easy being the youngest of fourteen children
even in the best of times. In the belly of the Great Depression, it would have been the greatest of hardships, but
Marco was only six months old when the market finally
crashed and he was more interested in his toes than stock
reports.

But he was a Depression kid insomuch as he never
knew what it was to have enough to eat and clothes

bought new just for him until the war came on in 1938 and offered jobs for all.

The Giambelli family had a way of happiness about them. They knew how to make a joke out of bitter disappointments, hard times, and personal tragedies. They even joked about the fact that, with so many kids yelling and screaming around the house, Marco was ten years old before anyone realized he couldn't talk or hear.

They said how lucky Marco was not to have to listen to the constant uproar around the place.

That wasn't true, of course. It was just a joke. Marco received special training at the city school for the handicapped from the time he was six years old. He could speak a mile a minute with his fingers by the time he was ten, and could read lips with fair expertise half a dozen years later.

When he grew into manhood, most people didn't know about his affliction, thought him shy and somehow wise in his silence. That's one of the fictions men live by. "Still waters run deep," and so on and so forth. On the other hand, when they found out he was a deaf-mute, they thought he was stupid. That's another fiction men live by. Humans haven't become truly enlightened. They've just learned the word.

Marco had a man's growth by the time he was sixteen. Just as well, for the war took all seven of his older brothers before the government got around to limiting the amount of blood and sacrifice one family could make. The family way of happiness died with the last of them. Old man Giambelli aged thirty years in thirty days.

He lost the light in his eyes and began to ail. It was no sickness of the body but of the spirit.

Nevertheless, it took the body's strength from him. He couldn't work at his trade as long or as hard as he once could. He was a carpenter and a brick layer.

Then he wasn't either, anymore.

His sons, but for Marco, were dead. His daughters, but for Tessa, married and making families of their own, and the old man was ready to die himself. And he did one day in the middle of May.

Marco arranged for the funeral and arranged for the sale of the big house. He settled his mother and Tessa into an apartment in the same neighborhood so they wouldn't have to make new friends. He kissed them both and, despite their tears, went off to join the Merchant Marines.

He saw what there was to see. His mates liked him. They would tell him tales when his eyes were elsewhere and in this way he served as confessor to the irreligious and lay analyst to the emotionally crippled. They poured out their troubled souls to the broad back of him and felt comforted for it. Sometimes, he turned around when one of them was in midconfession. He read their eyes and knew how afraid they were even though they immediately stopped off their mouths.

He had his deepest conversation with a dying man who'd been crushed by a falling crate on the docks of Tel Aviv. He'd lifted the heavy burden from the man's crushed chest single-handed. When he took the man in his arms, his own arms were trembling with the effort. As he gazed into the Jew's dark and grateful eyes—grateful to be held while dying—he felt his own chest contract upon itself as though it had been crushed. Felt it stagger in its breath against the restriction of some great weight. Looked into the dying man's eyes and saw the reflection of his own imminent death.

A doctor explained to him by signs and writing upon a prescription pad that he had suffered a heart attack. It was described as the result of coronary ischemia and the experienced pain as angina pectoris. Predisposing factors were smoking, obesity, hypertension, and a sedentary manner of life.

Marco smiled softly and joked with his eyes at the doctor, who shrugged his shoulders and laughed aloud. For, in his forty-second year, Marco did not smoke and had never done so. Neither did he drink wine to excess and drank nothing else at all. He was not fat by any means and his great strength was certainly some small evidence that his life was far from sedentary.

"Hypertension must be the villian," he wrote on the doctor's prescription pad and stared at him with admirable calm.

He left the sea because of that conversation he'd had with the dying Jew on the docks. The man who was—he later discovered—a displaced person from the Ukraine, told him with his eyes that he was dying far from home. That home*lands* were not home. The place of the heart alone was not home. It was heart and smell and the memory that is in touch and taste and sounds—even when there are no sounds to be remembered but only the sight of things that made them. Marco left the sea because he didn't want to die in some strange port as the Jew had, or in some strange land or on the breast of the sea itself.

He went home to Newark, New Jersey, to the flat where his mother and Tessa lived. He moved in with them and became the dutiful son.

His mother looked around to find a wife for him. Her friends had gone. The neighborhood had turned black. The world had turned while she wasn't looking. Marco let her know he wanted no wife but still she tried, writing letters to his sisters in other parts of the country, to her own sisters and brothers and to a hundred cousins scattered over the face of America and Italy. She was happy doing it. It gave her a reason to say hello to all the people she hadn't heard from in so long. Gave her reason to confront them with their neglect of her. See how she had never complained, would not complain even now? Nor ask for help? But this was not for herself. It was for Marco, come home from the sea and wanting a wife.

Marco found work in the great produce market that served the city. He was a valued employee because he could lift more than three men. He wasted no time gossiping. All in all, he was a worker raised to the worth of six workers.

He liked the loamy smell of celery with the dark earth still buried in the creases of the stems. He bit into tomatoes warm from the sun and was very well pleased. He ate watermelon cold and cob corn hot, cooked on the pierced steel drums that gave warmth to the early mornings of the autumn. He filled his mother's house with fruits and vegetables.

He bought a television set for her—and himself—enclosed in an ornate wooden cabinet. It was a joy and an amazement to him. He would watch and laugh because he didn't have to care about all the separate deaths he witnessed there.

In the silence of his mind, he had come to think of death without the attendant cacophony of grief. The word lay on his tongue, the sound and taste of the word. It was like the earth around the roots of vegetables, slightly sickening with the odor of decay but rich and robust all the same.

His mother died, suddenly in the night, and he cried for the first time at death and loss and doubt of immortality. He cried because he wanted to. Because it was a good thing.

His sister was quiet around him, for there was no sense to talk when she lived with a brother who couldn't hear.

She was a practical girl—forty-seven—was Tessa. A Mr. Lombardi, a widower, came calling.

He came every night for two weeks and Tessa fed him homemade Italian dishes. Marco sat with them and nodded and smiled as they spoke together. He wondered if Tessa was trying to snare Mr. Lombardi into marriage. If so, why had she waited so long before seeking a husband? For the sake of her mother? Perhaps. More likely she had no need of a husband when her mother was alive to speak with. If he could hear and talk, she probably wouldn't be looking for a husband now. But she was. That soon became clear.

He stayed away deliberately a few nights. This was to give Tessa an opportunity to show Mr. Lombardi she had gifts other than cooking and for him to show her that he had appetites for things other than fettucine. When a man and woman are very young and caught up in old-fashioned ways, they can defer bed until after marriage.

At least, that's the way it used to be. But when a certain age is past, they like to know there's good temper and fair skill before yoking up for the long haul.

Apparently, Tessa had learned a few lessons along the way. They announced their marriage and Marco looked around for a place to stay. He worried about it. He'd never really been alone ever in his life. The presence of other humans was always near.

It was on a day when he was giving it his deepest consideration while lifting several crates of cabbages, that a young man tapped him on the arm. Marco stood there holding the heavy weight and watched the fellow's lips.

The flashy, smiling talker was waving his hands—one was scarred and twisted—as he described the wonders of the open road and the pleasures of the carefree life. He turned away to gesture a path through the crates and

stacks of produce and his voice was, therefore, lost to
Marco. But he'd heard enough—read enough—to decide
it would be no bad way of life. Much like going out to sea,
going from port to port, with none of the danger of dying
out there on the breast of nowhere. If another attack or
any other illness took him, he would surely have time
enough to make his way back to the city of Newark,
changed as it was, and die within sight and smell of his
"neighborhood."

It was, wondrously, three days before Will Carney realized that the man he'd hired to do the heavy work and
perform as a Strong Man was a deaf-mute. Somehow, it
pleased him and he tried to reckon a way to make the
handicap work into an act of some sort, but no special
thought ever came to him. Enough, then, to bill him on
the canvas and the throwaways as "MARCO, THE SI-
LENT SAMSON."

Marco found Paulette and Serena wonders beyond
imagining, though he was put off by their imperfections.
The Colonel was another matter altogether. The nicely
molded figure of the little man fascinated him. He wondered if he would be buried, when he died, in a child's
coffin.

If so, he would carry it, and the little man inside it, all by
himself. He could not imagine why there was something
monumentally symbolic in the act when he thought of
doing it.

He dwelt upon the matter of his own death, and that of
others, quite frequently. But since he could never speak
of it to anyone, no one ever knew the terrible cast of his
thoughts.

People seemed so wild-eyed intent upon living when
death was mentioned or seemed near. They were, per-

haps, more afraid of it than he. At least, Marco seemed patient in the waiting for it. Fearing after his death and for his sick heart didn't change the Strong Man's ways one bit. Never had. Never would. Marco was glad in the great strength of his arms and legs. Glad in the silence and warmth when he took a woman to bed. Glad in most ways.

Now he sat bolt upright in the grip of the greatest pain of all. Whatever special fate had awaited him had come upon him now. It was a fitting end to a life that had been as strange as his own. Almost a dream ending, the mad girl that had begun this crazy night, the long, terrifying plunge down the mountain side, down into a black nowhere. It was clear from the first he'd been slated to die caught out on the empty breast of nowhere, far from home. Marco had once thought nowhere was a sea.

Now he knew it was a mountain.

Serena cried out involuntarily in the dark, her dream telling her more than she wanted then to know. She knew it was over for Marco, that in rendering Will Carney unconscious, Marco had performed the final task she had saved him for. She had hoped he could help them still more.

I am sorry, Serena. Marco's thoughts touched hers. It is my time and even you, with your strange wonders, can not hold me. I am going into the pain, the last pain.

Serena wept silently in the dark. Let me help you. I'll ease the pain. There will be no pain. I will make death love you.

And she went deeply inside him with her dream, shaping it for him and him alone, in his last minutes.

At Marco's feet the tawny sands ran to touch the softly lapping waves which stretched westward to be lost in the blue haze of the horizon. He stood in the curve of the bay, staring into infinities of distance as absolute as the view.

He seemed to be waiting for a ship. He sensed that was his purpose for being there. The sun shone as if it were the first day of the world. There was a sense of strangeness and wonder. Of wrongness, too, but it did not seem important. It was not quite the world he lived in, but it seemed a fair world.

With the silent wind came the long ship, oars sweeping it in a headlong rush toward the beach.

Marco looked down at himself and found himself dressed in a rough, woolen toga and heavy, leather armor. His right hand held a short sword of burnished metal. On his feet were rough sandals of crude design.

Now that was strange, very strange, but no stranger than the ship that made for the beach, a ship the like of which had not been seen upon the sea for hundreds of years.

And the man on the deck, that was Will Carney and it was not. The man waved at him, motioned him forward. He yelled but the words were lost in the wind.

Marco found himself marching into the sea. The water was warm as a kiss and blue as the sky. He stumbled through the waves.

Strong arms took him from the water, lifted him up into the ship.

Pepino was there, with a shy grin on his face. And fat Paulette. And Colonel John in a toga just his size. The faces of the crew were those of strangers and yet they were not strangers.

The ship whirled around like a graceful swan, heading out to sea. The sail, blood red, sprang up the mast, pulled by unseen hands.

The wind caught her full and the ship went speeding across the waves like a dragonfly.

It was a thing of wonder and Marco wanted very much to say so, but of course he could not speak nor could he hear. It was all a dream. He knew that, but, somehow, he expected to hear, to talk. Wouldn't that be the fitting end, to have what one was so long denied in the end?

And where was fair Serena? He looked in vain for her in the silent faces of the crew.

And the ship sailed off into the great mystery of the sea. And the strong man stood before the mast, hearing neither the crash of waves against the bow or the cries of the men who manned her.

That seemed sad, somehow, and he missed Serena terribly.

The wind felt good on Marco's face and the sun was a warmth that burned into him. The clean, sea air was as good as life itself.

It was a bright and beautiful dream, a wonderful going away. Marco knew it for what it was.

If only I could hear, if only the dream were complete.

Will Carney came up beside him, the man that might be Will Carney, and he held a stout length of rope in his hands. The man who looked like Pepino came up and took one end of the rope. With his other hand, he pushed gently on Marco's chest until he was forced to step back. His back came up against the mast.

He felt no urge to resist. There was a rightness about everything that happened. Marco sensed that.

With the rope, they lashed Marco tightly against the mast.

And then Marco saw that the ears of the men were stopped up with white candle wax.

And thus they came speeding across the waves toward the dark island.

Marco strained against the ropes then, feeling restless, but not knowing quite why. Something was happening.

The island was an isle of dreams and crystal and white mist. On the shore, beautiful maidens danced and threw flowers into the blue water. Fairest of them all, was a girl. No, not a girl, Serena, the queen of them all, tall and fair and like pale fire in her beauty.

And she sang, and the sirens joined her in that song and it was the rarest and most wondrous of all sounds. Marco alone heard it, alone felt it tearing its way into his mind and heart. It was a song meant only for him and it was summer and fire and ice and a thousand sounds he had never heard. It was all he had ever imagined or ever dreamed. It was the cry of sea birds in rapture and the laughter of children and the hum and keening of a thousand animal and human voices.

It was the sound of love and pleasure and joy and the endless sighing of the sea and the ceaseless tides.

It was the sound of his own heartbeat, the sound of his struggle against the ropes that bound his chest, the sound of spring and the end of night.

Beautiful Serena, he had found her at last.

A siren singing ever so sweetly in his going away.

And the sound of his own pain was as sweet as any human voice. Like the song that could not be resisted, like the song that touched everything that ever had been in him, the pain flared like a great, shattered crystal in his chest.

Marco slumped against the ropes that bound him, against the pain.

And the song was the sun in his face and the wind in his hair that stayed within him, until the mighty heart gave out.

It had been a truly wonderful going away.

Will came to with a far-off cry ringing in his ears. He came
awake to the feeling of something heavy pushing against
him. He opened his eyes and saw the rain sweeping past
the window. Marco was leaning into him. It was Marco
trying to push him out of the truck to fall down to the
rocks below where he'd be smashed to his death. He
fought back against the weight of the mute. They were,
for a long while, locked in silent combat. He turned his
head to shout the Strong Man away. He looked into
Marco's slitted eyes and then saw the jaw agape, the
tongue lolling from it. He screamed out in terrible fear.
He was being embraced and shoved to his destruction by
a dead man.

"So you're finally awake, are you, Will?" the Colonel
said almost perkily.

Will pushed steadily against the dead weight. Marco
came slowly upright and then slid slowly backward into
the seat like a man settling to rest his weary bones. His
head tipped back, the mouth still open, tongue out like a
tired hound's. The eyes were opened slightly and cocked
a look at Will.

"Goddamnit, Will. Speak up. We need some tool for me
to work on the ventilator. There's a screwdriver in there.
Give it to me."

Obediently, Will bent over and scrabbled around on
the floor with his good hand, keeping his eyes on Marco all

the while, for fear the dead man would attack him again.
The cab tilted a fraction and Marco's head nodded a bit, as
though agreeing that such an attack was in his mind. Will
found the screwdriver and, straightening back up in the
seat, handed it over his shoulder through the communication window.

"Drop it," the Colonel said and Will did.

"Marco's dead," Will said, as though by way of conversation.

"Are you that drunk, man?"

"I am most sober. I wish that I *were* drunk."

The Colonel looked at his companions. They had all
heard the news. Paulette touched her eyes and found
tears to wet her fingertips. Pepino had no tears, being a
philosopher, but he felt a tightness in his throat, a lump as
big as his heart.

The Midget glanced at Serena, who placed her beautiful hands together as though in prayer and touched her
lips with the tips of her fingers.

When he handed the screwdriver to Pepino, his hands
shook. The Colonel did not want to believe it.

"You're that drunk, Will."

"Marco's dead, I tell you. His eyes are glazed open and
his lips are blue," insisted Will.

The Colonel bowed his head, grieving for his lost friend,
for a mountain of strength that had so often in the past
been offered to him as strength when his small size gave
him none.

The Rubber Man inserted the blade of the screwdriver
under the lip of the ventilator flange. He pried gently and
it gave, dropping little flecks of paint and rust into his
eyes.

"Goddamn," he said, and shook his head. He cleared his
eyes with his fingers and went back to work. Delicately,
he pried all around the flange until the ring that held it in

place became loose. There were a half dozen screws in the flange that held the tubular column of the shaft. They were eaten away with rust. The slots for the driver blade could scarcely be found.

Holding his arms high above his head and working without really being able to see, Pepino started first one, then another, of the screws. There was the constant fear that the corroded metal would crumple clear away and give no purchase for the screwdriver blade. But it held.

Pepino's hair and the shoulders of his shirt were dusted with rust, which gleamed, even in the faint yellow light, like the wind-blown dust of Mars.

He got his fingers beneath the lip of the second flange and pulled the whole shaft out like the cork out of an upside-down bottle.

Pepino turned his head around and grinned at the Colonel. It was a grimace of pain, instead.

"What's the matter?" the Colonel asked immediately.

"Arms hurt like hell."

"Rest a little."

Pepino lowered his arms and twisted his torso. The pain did not stop.

"The mountain is shuddering," Serena said very matter-of-factly.

Spurred on, Pepino stretched his arms up high again and removed the guts of the ventilator, the spindle, and the vanes. The cap, shaped like a mushroom, was easily pushed aside, then. It clattered on the roof and bounced once or twice before plunging over the side.

"What was that?" Will cried out.

"That was Pepino opening up our way out of here," said the Midget.

"What do you mean? Tell me what you're doing?"

"We've got the top off the ventilator, Will. I'm going out now," said the Colonel.

"Oh, thank God, thank God!"

"No, Will, thank the damned Juggler." The Colonel laughed.

"What are you laughing about? You tell me. You mean to leave me here? You mean to get out and save yourself and leave me here?"

"Leave you, Will?"

"Leave all of us!" screamed Will. "Don't help him! Don't any of you help him!"

The Colonel only laughed by way of reply. He smiled at Pepino.

Pepino took his place beneath the open port in the roof. He lifted the Midget first to his chest, like a child held to a parent's breast, then to his shoulder. The Colonel stepped up on the Rubber Man's shoulders and reached up. Pepino lifted him overhead, his muscles protesting with the strain.

The Colonel's tiny finger caught the outside rim and he pulled himself up and out into the rain. He turned at once and popped his head back into the van for a moment.

"I'm going to open the door in back now. Don't move. We've still got to clear all those goods out of the way."

"Colonel John," Pepino said, looking up at him.

The Colonel waited for what Pepino had to say.

"Do what you can, Colonel, but if you can't do it in time, save yourself."

The Colonel wasted no time playing at promises. He nodded and disappeared from the hole that now let fresh air into the truck. If they were to die now, at least, it would be with the sweet smell of rain in their mouths.

The Colonel didn't trust the leather of his heels and shoes on the rain-slick steel roof. He feared a long, skidding slide. So he clung like a limpet and slid on his belly like a snail. The wind gusted at times and he clung, then, with his knees and fingernails. When the wind got at him, almost lifting him off the roof, he tried to make himself smaller. If the wind caught him on the move, he would be sped to his death. He made his way by inches, all the while wanting to move as fast as a sprinter leaping off the starting blocks.

Inside the van, Pepino looked at Paulette and then at Serena, who seemed to be looking back at him, as well. It was very plain that they all felt monstrously afraid, now that the little tactician was gone. He might be small but he had been, apparently, large enough to be their heart.

The Colonel found his way to the tail of the truck. Eyebolts used to lash down tarpaulins gave him foot- and handholds. He swung down upon them like a Barbary ape.

When his toes touched the slight ledge that accommodated the width of the hinges of the ramp, he paused and reached out toward the hook that secured the hasp. He lifted it and dropped it free, then inched his way along until he reached the hook and chain at the other end. He flung that free, as well.

Now he returned to the center and the sliding bolt that locked the ramp. He grasped it with both his small hands and lifted it so that it would be free of the notches. He hadn't far to go now. He would slide the blot and leap away as the ramp fell.

He grinned in anticipation of the daring rescue he was effecting. He froze midmotion.

Were he to drop the tailgate ramp, the entire contents might well tumble out, destroying the delicate balance, and the truck and all in her would plunge away to death.

He clung there in the rain and felt the deepest despair.

"I need your wonderful hands again, Serena."

"The mountain's going to collapse any minute," she said, and her voice rose to the edge of breaking. Will's keening stopped abruptly as though sensitive to her fear, as though waiting to hear the oracle give expression to the certainty of their doom.

The Colonel hurried over to her and took her ghostly head in his arms. He pulled her to him so that her cheek lay upon his chest. He rumbled soothingly.

"Whatever, whatever. We're together, aren't we? I can't imagine things being any other way. Come on, now. We'll try."

Serena smiled. In some way, she understood that no dream of hers could have made John do as he had done. If she had made him a giant in a dream, he had already made himself a giant of the human heart. She understood that Colonel John was a fighter and that he loved them all and fought all the harder. Perhaps she had only made him aware of what he was.

With great care, the Colonel and Pepino rearranged the Moon Child close beside the remaining barrier to freedom. Serena shivered at the chill column of air that came into the space and smiled.

"How good and clean it feels," she said. She placed her hands upon the faces of boxes and bales.

The Midget and the Rubber Man placed their hands and their strength where she bade them.

"What are you doing? What are you doing?" Will very nearly screamed, and started to turn about in the cab, fearing that they had already managed their escape and left him behind. His flailing arm struck the taut extension cord of the worklamp and tore it from the cigarette lighter.

Darkness descended, more startling than lightning.

Inside the van, Pepino sat down close to Paulette and prepared to die. It was all very well to cheerfully pretend to hope but a wise man recognized an impossible situation when he saw one.

Serena felt Colonel John's despair like a knife upon her consciousness, but there was nothing she could do. She was exhausted past effort.

Colonel John looked up toward the top of the mountain and whatever God was beyond the peak.

The rain stopped suddenly. The air was still filled with spray but the weight of the rain was past. The Colonel smiled, for he took the cessation of the rain as a sign.

He jumped back, releasing the pin and the tailgate fell with a bang. A box of light bulbs tumbled out, smashing on the rocks. They burst with small explosions. Nothing else in the welter of goods jammed against the tailgate moved.

He examined the complexity and chose a carton that might be safely removed. He uttered small prayers as he slipped it from its place in the general tumble. A few things slipped and slid but one motion counterbalanced another and the truck remained secure upon it's split ledge.

"Is it you, Colonel?" Pepino shouted. "I saw something move at the back. Is it you?"

"It's me. It's me," the Colonel shouted back, with laughter and hope rich in his voice.

Suddenly, almost without warning, the mountain shifted, freeing a great slab of earth and rock. Inside the van, Serena threw her arms up toward a dream that was no longer there as she felt the truck move crazily, settling itself for its death plunge.

"Oh yes, *my God!*" Paulette shouted, as though witnessing for Christ at a tent meeting.

Pepino turned to face the two women and stretched out his arms as though to embrace them and keep them safe.

In the cab, Will Carney let out a scream that would have wakened all the spirits of the mountain had there been any left there, sheltered from the storm in her caves and hidey-holes.

That part of the road upon which the front wheel so precariously clung rose up as the ledge was split in two. The mountain stirred like an old, malevolent beast shifting from one leg to another, seeking rest.

Boxes, bales, bundles of cloth, rods and ropes and pulleys and show banners came tumbling out the tailgate in a rush. Several struck the Colonel but, in the first moment of the mountain's heaving, the little man had leapt back, as though hoping to make it seem that his own death fall was deliberate, that he was not—small as he was—victim of a power greater than he. He lay bruised on the wet, muddy earth and was struck with the awe of yet another miracle. Not only did the van still cling marvelously to the mountainside, but the rise of the forward ground, the tumbling of the packages, had done much of his work for him.

He could see through the welter of goods deep into the interior of the van where the glow of the worklamp created a yellow pool of light in the dark.

He scrambled to his feet and went to the tailgate, peering through the tunnel created by the variety of things.

"Everyone all right in there?"

"Yes, everyone's fine, Colonel," Pepino answered.

Will's initial scream had settled into a mad, high-pitched keening.

"Perhaps not," Pepino amended.

"Can you make it through the space?" the Colonel asked.

Pepino's face suddenly appeared at the other end of the short tunnel. He tried to force his shoulders through the beginning of the passageway.

"I might make it through but I doubt it."

"Stay back. I'm coming inside again," the Colonel ordered.

"Wait," Pepino said softly. "Do you think that's wise?"

"We've got to widen the space. I think it can be done more easily from inside than out."

"You'd do better to take yourself away," Pepino advised.

But the Colonel was already up on the tailgate and down on his knees. He crawled back through to them, feeling the trembling of the mountain through the palms of his hands. He wondered if his nerves were making him as sensitive to things as Serena was.

"It won't be long now. Just a little more work, then we'll all be out," he assured them.

Serena, totally spent, was beginning to doubt even her dreams. Then, too, she was steadily feeling increasing tremors from the mountain, an indication that the end was very near.

"The ledge on which the truck is resting is ready to go at any moment," said Serena. "We've run out of time."

"Go back, Colonel, and save yourself. Go back," Pepino added.

Paulette nodded and a small sob caught in her throat.

The Colonel came all the way into the van and stood

Pepino and the Colonel froze with a large carton held between them.

The mountain shrugged at the foolishness of small creatures.

The dark was as thick and cold and bone chilling as sea water. And like the sea that drowns, it recalled, in flashes, scenes of Will Carney's sorry life, unwinding before his eyes in little acts without beginnings or endings.

He saw his father at the picnic of his death. Willy had been ten and his father seemed tall as a tree and stronger than any man alive. He had red hair and a wide mouth filled with big, dead-white teeth like cheap, broken crockery. He liked to tell everybody what a great fellow he was when he had enough beer or whiskey in him. That hot day he had more than enough. Drunkenly, he boasted of his strength and his boxing skills. He stuck out his chest, strutted like a rooster, and told one and all that he had bedded every pretty girl in the county. It was the whiskey talking and almost everyone knew it.

Hiram Weeks, just married to a girl of the county—at the unrefusable request of her father and his shotgun—in his own drunken state, reckoned that Big Red Carney was insulting his own fair bride. Thinking that, he stepped up behind Big Red and punched him in the back of the neck.

Will's father fell forward like a steer hammered between the eyes with a sledge.

The hoop of a beer keg caught him squarely across the forehead. He was dead before he hit the ground.

That left young Will alone since his ma had left Big Red's bed and board—such as it was—along with his drunken anger and heavy hand, half a dozen years before.

There was one hell of a lot of commotion about the death. There was a coroner's inquest. The killing was deemed accidental. Moments after—since all the town officials were gathered for the hearing anyway—the people took up the matter of the recently orphaned boy.

Hiram Weeks, found innocent of any murder or wrongdoing—except perhaps an excess of Fourth of July zeal—felt himself responsible for losing Will his father. He charitably offered to take the boy in. To feed, clothe, school, and teach him a trade at his own expense.

Within a week, young Will, who recognized slavery when he saw it, ran off to live in and around town, catch as catch can.

And then Abner Wesker and the wonders of juggling.

And then sixteen and Abner, falling on Will's knife for nothing, for a girl who belonged to no one, for an unownable nothing. And then off on his own. An endless, unending tumble through cheap hotels and boarding houses. Painted faces and eyes too artfully wide to be innocent, nameless joinings.

Sometimes one step ahead of the law, that was carnival. Sometimes one step ahead of a jealous husband or irate boyfriend, that was Will's lot. Nothing held him for long, no faces in the dark, no hearth or home in anybody's face he ever met.

The pictures kept going faster before his eyes, a nickel-

odeon gone mad. In the dark on the black mountain, Will
put up his hand to turn off the crazy projector. This was no
way to look at a life, swift and in pieces. A life should be
looked at in a leather-bound picture book. One remembered moment at a time. Tasting and savoring each pho-
tograph for the good and the wonder and the glory that
was in it. But the machine kept rolling his life past him
and the people ran in and out so fast he couldn't remember their faces or the touch of them. He couldn't remember their names. He could barely remember his own small
hopes.

Someplace along the way, he learned to read fairly well.
Mostly comic books with the adventures of Captain Marvel and Plastic Man described within the multicolored
covers.

He graduated from comic books to little dirty books,
badly illustrated pornography that featured inept paro-
dies of Maggie and Jiggs and Moon Mullins—still around
after all those years. He also read proper books from time
to time, and once came across a life of P. T. Barnum.

From that moment on, he no longer saw himself as a
rag-tag, wandering juggler, a knight without armor walking down the long, dusty highway. Where once he had
considered himself rich if two coins clinked together in
his pocket, he now clothed himself a much more expensive and ambitious dream. From that day on, he aspired
to, once and for all, to be an impresario, an entrepreneur.
He looked up both words in a dictionary and found them
pleasing and accurate to the naming of his desires.

The book was read and the ambition formed about the
time that Will was quartering the Southwest in an old '59
panel truck, selling what junk he could, enjoying what
beds became available to him and juggling in his fairly

sorry way. It became the commandment of his dreams and shone there before his eyes when he took Paulette under his management and set out on the road to bigger things.

He quickly gathered up Pepino where he'd dropped him in Wilmington, Pennsylvania, after a quarrel over the sharing out of a windfall won in a poker game, and sketched out the picture of the future he'd already come to treasure. Truth was, the quarrel had been all one-sided. Greedily, Will had decided to cheat Pepino and use the winnings to buy the truck and the merchandise to set himself off on a career as a merchant prince. Now, Pepino and his quiet willingness were needed. His freakish talent to dislocate his bone joints was useful to the creation of a proper sideshow.

He found Pepino working for a greengrocer not half a dozen doors away from the saloon where they'd had their parting of the ways. Will had known he would be close by, for Pepino had no ambitions, goals, or any place to go. He found the sad-eyed philosopher picking through a crate of bruised tomatoes as though he were an archeologist sorting the shards of some ancient civilization's pottery.

"Come along, come along, Pepino." Will smiled as he chose three tomatoes and sent them bounding about through the air in clever rhythmic patterns.

"I think not," said Pepino. "I've had enough of the open roads and doubtful rooming houses and. . . ." Pepino hesitated for a second, before completing the thought. "And enough of you, as well, Will Carney."

"But what will you do?" asked Will, his eyes on the tomatoes in the air.

Pepino stared at the speeding objects as a snake stares at a charmer's moving flute. "I'll get by."

"Will you? Ah, no, Pepino, old friend. You need something to suffer for, something to be forbearing about, some pain to endure."

"No."

"And someone to care about," added Will. "In your patient and saintly and forgiving way."

"Well, then, I must find someone else, for I surely can't care for a bully and a cheat like you."

Will laughed and knew in his heart he already had Pepino in his pocket. "You can suffer my faults and forgive me often for the good of your own soul. Come along and be part of my great Carnival and Sideshow. Come along and meet the Fabulous Fat Girl, Paulette!"

Pepino came along.

There was a girl with blond hair named Susy in Charleston, West Virginia. Why such thoughts of such a girl—one casual companion among so many—should come so startlingly clear to his mind, Will wondered. The film of his memory rolled on without control, as if the projectionist was dead and the ushers asleep. But the memory was there, sharp and vivid, whether Will liked it or not. He knew he had not remembered her name ten minutes after she'd left the sorry room he'd rented for the length of that vaudeville engagement so long ago? Did it mean she had been someone of great importance to him and he never knew it at the time, until now, on the dark side of a mountain with destiny shouting at him?

In the rerun of that time back when, Will grumblingly put his bare feet on the worn carpet and toddled to the door to see who the hell was bothering his afternoon matinee. He opened the door a crack and the little man came barreling through. The girl Susy screamed in the bed. Oh yes, he had forgotten her name in the sudden intention that came to him of signing up the midget as part of his great Carnival.

That was the reason for remembering that girl named Susy, for she was the means of bringing Colonel John to his troupe. He was young and whole then, was Will Carney. Two hands useful to him, hands that boasted certain skills and the hope of a great future shining in his greedy eyes. And, too, he had the gift of a silver tongue, the means to charge other people with his own dreams.

Hadn't he talked a deaf strong man into joining him?

Hadn't he charmed a blind girl into coming along?

Yes, he had done that and more, but they had come to him and shared the dream after the dream was faded and all but gone. They'd come too late to enjoy the happy Will Carney, with the foxy eyes and tricky fingers. Five of those fingers were maimed and the final bitterness of Will's life had set in.

Pepino and the Colonel stood poised, with the heavy carton held between them, for a long, long moment. Then, suddenly whispering to one another so as not to further alarm the others, they lowered the box to the floor of the van.

Only then did the Colonel give way to his fear and his anger.

"What the hell have you done with the light, Will Carney? What the hell have you done to kill us all?"

There was no answer, for Will was even then reliving the short reels of his life.

The Midget made his way to the partition between van and cab, moving his feet slowly across the floor.

"Tell me, Serena, if the truck shifts or slides or even threatens to," he reminded her.

She breathed some response but whether it was a portion of her strange dreams or a sigh, could not be determined.

The Colonel reached those boxes he'd piled up once before when last he'd tried to find a way out through the cab. He climbed them carefully. As carefully as a turtle sticking out his head sensing danger, the Colonel extended the top half of himself into the cab.

At that moment, stagey, showy, and frightening in its way, the clouds parted and the bright, full moon shone down upon the mountain.

The Colonel saw Will sitting there with his lips moving as though reading the captions upon a screen, following the little bouncing ball of a Saturday-night sing-along. The Colonel touched his shoulder and Will started as though touched by the hand of a living nightmare.

He uttered a short scream, staring pop-eyed at the body of the Strong Man. In the light of the moon, Marco's mouth seemed caught in a horrible smile of welcome.

"You've taken away our light, you damn fool," the Colonel told Will.

Will shook his head in refutation to what, in response to what, only he, God, and the Juggler knew.

The Colonel dimly saw the tangle of the lamp's extension cord upon the floor. He pointed at it past Will's shoulder.

"We need that light. Pick it up but go easy at it."

Will continued to shake his head. He smiled as though trying to match the smile upon Marco's face and thereby placate and please the corpse.

The Colonel slapped Will awkwardly upon the cheek. "Move, you fool. Move!"

Will smiled and nodded his head and otherwise remained immobile.

"What's the matter with Will?" Pepino's voice asked. It was close by. When the Colonel skewed his head around he saw the Rubber Man standing in the van just behind him.

"He's in shock or something or other."

"Is Marco truly dead?"

There was a slight quaver in John's voice. "Yes. There seems no doubt of it."

The Colonel returned his glance to Will, who continued to nod his head like one of those queerly disturbing mechanical dolls with fatuous grins that, once set in motion by the touch of a finger, seemed to converse with some unseen presence.

"Will?" he ventured again, in a soft voice, and then gave it up altogether. Once again he turned his head round and peered back into the body of the truck. The moonlight seemed to flow down through the circular hole left by the removed ventilator.

The shaft of limpid light bathed Serena's white hair and gave it the milky cast of moonstone. Her face was turned up to it. Her shapely hands were still lifted so that they rested against the boxes.

Serena seemed in some strange state of communication with a moon goddess that was her mother. Her eyes, startingly, seemed sighted and she smiled a secret, soft smile.

"Is there enough light to see by, do you think?" the Colonel asked Pepino.

"For the moment, but what if the clouds should cover the moon again?"

"As it will most likely do when we're least prepared for it," the Colonel agreed. "Well, there's nothing else for it," he said with resignation. "Let's hope the truck has dug itself in a bit more."

He boosted himself with his short arms. He shoved his shoulders against the surrounding chicken wire and shattered glass. He thrust his way through and felt the sharp wire ends and glass edges claw at him.

When he was at last through, he poised like an organ grinder's monkey on the back of the cab seat. He took a shuddering gasp through his open mouth and became aware that he'd been holding his breath for a long while.

He felt no trembling, no movement of the precariously balanced structure. No whispered command to stop moving had come from the alert, although exhausted Moon Child.

Colonel John slipped down between Will and the body of Marco.

"Take care. Take care," Serena crooned, as though calling to a lover.

The Colonel shifted his position away from Will. In that direction overbalance and disaster lay. He grasped the shoulders of the corpse and gently eased himself down Marco's body to the floor as though descending a mountain. The flesh, where he touched it, seemed warm, yet cold beneath. It was soft yet rigid with approaching rigor mortis.

The Midget was much afraid. The body shifted and the hair on his head rose in atavistic terror. One of Marco's arms shifted as though to embrace him and it was all the Colonel could manage to keep from leaping away in mindless escape.

Will had stopped the ceaseless nodding and was looking sideways at the midget and at the corpse. Had he seen Marco's movements? And having seen them, would new terror cause him to panic and kill them all?

"It's all right, Will. It's only me. It's all right," the Colonel said.

Will smiled. There was no grace or charm to it. It gave no trace of kindliness to his face. The Colonel wondered why they, all of them, had ever allowed this creature to be the master of their lives.

If he could hear the truth spoken—that love was the cement that held them all—Colonel John would not have believed it.

It would seem that Will Carney was not far off the mark when he laughed at Pepino's refusal to return to him for more contempt and ill-usage. He recognized in the Romany soul of Pepino the need for martyrdom. The punishment Pepino sought was not for any sins of his own, but, Christ-like, for the sins of the world. Had there been some ritual manner in which the Rubber Man might have been tied to a cross at Eastertime, he would have accepted the role of the Messiah. But not, however, if the rite must include the reality of spikes driven into hands and feet or the spear driven into his side. In casting about for a suitable penance to pay for the transgressions of mankind, he had Will Carney, who was evil enough in the least painful of ways.

Upon the arrival of the others—the Fat Girl, the Midget, the deaf-mute Strong Man—Pepino began to gain a sense of that family which he'd once felt mad to escape from.

Paulette loved because it was in her nature to do so as it had been in her mother's. She loved everyone and would have been willing to prove it to all in any way that was asked of her. In the presence of her mother, she was bothered by the resentful feeling that she had been allowed, indeed urged, to grow monstrous so that she would be little competition to the woman who bore her. Or perhaps, more terribly, Paulette's mother had decided to make of her the living expiation of her own carnal sins. Sexuality lived in the huge bulk of her daughter but there was little expectation that it would ever be actively called upon. Had her own mother created a nun wedded to the chastity of flesh?

Was it possible, then, that Paulette had seen in the brash, grinning carnival man—the errant juggler with the flashing eyes—a certain promise that excited her own dreams of unattained love? Did a part of her still hold to a dream—lingering in her breast—in which some impossible diet was so severe it would make her desirable to Will?

Whatever, in her dreams she hoped for and desired Will. Once, when Will was drunk, he had even asked her to take her clothes off in front of him. As she had somewhat shyly started to comply, Will at first laughed at the fun of it, but then choked in disgust at what he was about. He made her stop and said evil things to her that made her cry even as her heart stilled from the passion that might have awoken in her.

Afterwards, there followed a long period when Will sometimes looked at her out of the corner of his eyes as though wondering whether or not she would demand something of him for some ill-considered promise, given when he was confused and unaware.

Paulette, too, accepted the traveling sideshow as her family. She sublimated her desires, blushed, pleased beyond measure by the fond and outrageous compliments paid her by the Colonel, the soft, kind regard of the Rubber Man, and the hands—so often holding hers comfortingly—those of her special love, Serena, the magical woman-child, who lived as one, giant heart for them all.

Serena, herself, loved Will Carney for the imperfection of him. She had from the first—as she had revealed to the good doctor and guardian so many years ago—read the pettiness and small evils in Will's face with her all-seeing fingers.

Had she hoped to save the man's soul and, in some way, prove her own reason for living? She did not quite know.

Her gentleness and patience had done nothing to alter Will's selfish and painful need to ridicule and belittle them all. She understood that, in her saintly way—different than the saint-search of Pepino—and she also accepted his apparent disregard of her. Deep inside herself, where dreams unlocked their secrets, she had the feeling, both power-giving and uncomfortable, that Will was drawn to her. She sensed a great fascination in him for her and, with it, an even greater and darker terror. Something atavistic in his bones and blood cried back, sensing witchcraft and rites performed in dark woodlands when the moon was full and night creatures stalked the nightland.

Will was afraid of her, and, to prove that he was not, he often treated her cruelly.

If not love that held them in thrall to the flawed, all-too-human, and sometimes magicless Merlin that was the Juggler, what else could it be. If not for love, why else would they have accepted his abuse?

"Without me you are nothing but a passel of freaks, a stupid collection of old bones and crippled bodies worth not a penny for your wage. I make you something. Gathering you up and putting you all together makes you something. I make you something! I did that!"

Perhaps he was right.

In the final accounting, whatever brought them together on the side of the mountain—pride, shame, remorse, greed, desire, hope, or love—they were, in the special circumstance and for this one moment in all their lives, uniquely suited, in their physical differences, to be their own heroes and saviours. And they had a dream to follow in which they saw themselves, strong in each of their special ways.

All but one of them who was already dead.

All but the one who was only slightly maimed, for he was most nearly without handicap and, therefore, most nearly useless.

Colonel John shook himself, steeling himself for the rest of the adventure. Choosing the space available nearest the door, he slid down Marco's stiffening legs, alert to any sound of protest from the truck. He kept his ears tuned to the call of his human seismograph, Serena.

Upon the floor of the cab, he reached out and then extended his hand an inch at a time until his fingers closed on one of the loops of the extension cord.

The truck heaved with a sickening jerk and the Colonel froze, his head tilted up to the top of the cab, away from ultimate destruction.

Serena called out but there was no need of it. The new evidence of their peril was known to them all.

The Midget reared back, imagining that even the small weight of his head and trunk would restore the delicate balance. Indeed, it seemed to do so.

The moon passed behind a cloud. Dark descended, with its ability to terrify the poor, trapped creatures in the truck. Will let out a soft, strangled cry as though his senses had roused in pain.

Colonel John manipulated his fingers so the cord traveled through his hand until he had the plug.

"The mountain is trembling," Serena called out.

The Colonel, with fear in his heart, lifted up one hand to reinsert the plug.

"Don't move!" cried Serena, sensing some convulsion.

The Colonel froze there in the dark, having no idea how far away the receptacle for the plug might be, a foot or only a few scant inches. Dare he reach that bit farther?

The moon reappeared just as he was about to retreat and give up the chancing of it. His fingers were only inches from the panel of the cab, the plug a hair's breadth from contact. With shaky fingers, he pushed it home. The moon disappeared as the light of the worklamp came on.

Carefully, the Colonel retraced his steps, making his way up the human alp that was the body of Marco. He climbed the legs, gained the mesa of the lap, and cautiously as any challenger of Everest, moved up the torso until he gained the dead man's shoulder. From that vantage, he found purchase and the way back through the small window.

He carried the precious lamp with him and brought its comfort with him, too. The simple restoration of the light seemed to lift everyone's spirits.

"Well, let's have at it once again, shall we?" the Colonel said.

Serena placed her hands once again upon the boxes, bales, and things. Pepino and the Colonel labored to clear the last few obstructions from the tunnel that would allow even the largest of them to escape. It was already wide enough to give safe passage to Pepino and Serena, as well as the Colonel. But they would not stop, despite the danger to them all, until it would be wide enough for Paulette, as well.

A torrential finger of water broke through, high up on the face of the mountain, pushing aside the boulders and debris that had impeded it. The finger of rapidly moving water branched out and became a three-fingered hand, rushing down the face of the mountain. That hand would crush and tear away the sheer side of the mountain.

Hands are tools and the pride of jugglers of all persuasions.

Will Carney felt the same way about his hands as did all pool sharks, card and dice mechanics, musicians and surgeons. Without the full use of them, life lost most of its meaning.

Just as no violinist should also be a prize fighter— Paulette wept over that film many a time—or no magician should try to bottom-deal a deck of cards in a big-money game, no juggler should let his hands get the better of him with someone else's property. In Will's case, his hands had touched a young girl in the wrong places at the wrong time.

And from that came the damage to his left hand, that maimed and scarred claw that was now all but useless in the pursuit of that skill of juggling which he once so proudly possessed.

The four of them—Will, Pepino, Paulette, and Colonel John—Serena and Marco had not yet joined their little band—found themselves stranded and broke on the outskirts of a farm community no more than two streets long and one street wide somewhere in the south of the great state of Pennsylvania. The fringe of the town was as far as they got before the battered Plymouth station wagon ran out of gas.

This failure of their transport irked Will no end, for it was a basic rule of his that the sharpie had to come upon his marks with every indication he was riding the crest of success and had need of neither money nor favor. To enter walking in the dust was to invite disaster. Walking in alone, he would have made no brave show of well-being to be afoot. With his freaks in tow, it was worse, far worse.

Whereas Paulette gained a certain grandeur from the simple act of rising from a chair, it was quite another story to see her panting and puffing as she made her painful way even a few yards. The great effort of walking brought sheens of sweat to her body which shamed her and made her seem disheveled and slovenly.

It was no great help to the image of success to see the Colonel trotting along beside her, his little hands raised as though to catch her if she toppled. It made for a comic thought about what would happen if, indeed, she did trip and fell on the little man.

The arrival, even in so small a place as this, had to be done with a certain flair. With a hat tipped jauntily over one eyebrow and a spring that spoke of well-being in every step. The bar of the best hotel should be sought out. Failing such an amenity, then the local tavern—there was always a tavern, no matter how small the crossroad—was the place to set up shop. The wares Will had to sell sold best when he could trade a ready smile, an air of hail-fellow-well-met, and lively conversation sprinkled with off-color jokes and his pair of clever hands.

As Will considered all this while standing beside the car, with one foot perched on the running board and staring at the gas cap as though it might perform some miracle for the hoping, he became aware of someone peering at him from afar.

A house stood well back from the road. From the shadows of the porch, a figure in white stood watching them. The little house had none of the raggedy air of the rest of the dwellings and stores. There was a certain Victorian grace about it and the porch even had four supporting pillars that looked vaguely Roman. The shadows were violet in color and gave the appearance of being cool and otherworldly. Will was suddenly filled with a longing for the kinds of summers he'd heard and read about but had never really known.

Breezes coming off small lakes and ponds. Picnics filled with gaudy bunting and laughter. His eyes misted over and he imagined he heard the tinkle of cracked ice in tall glasses filled with lemonade.

Will turned to see the figure in white, a girl, standing by the side of the automobile, a tray with a pitcher and four glasses upon it in her hands. Will hurried around the car to join her just as she murmured an invitation to Paulette and Pepino to refresh themselves.

The Colonel stepped out of the car and the girl gasped in wonder and delight, then colored in some confusion. Will guessed she hadn't seen the little man at all till now, and had brought only enough glasses for herself and those she had seen. Thirsty as he was, Will refused, raising his slender hands and insisting he had not thirst but "thank you very much all the same."

It was no nicety of manners that led him to do that. Will knew elaborate courtesy was the confidence man's best defence.

The drinks were wonderfully refreshing. The girl set the tray and pitcher down on the hood of the car and drank her lemonade pretty fast, then filled the glass again and handed it to Will.

"I think you were just being polite and I should have said I'd already had some on the porch."

"But you wanted to be friendly and drink with the strangers," Will grinned.

The girl colored again and said, "Well, then, you be friendly, too."

"Oh, I will, I will." He took the lemonade and downed it and smacked his lips with just the right emphasis, not so loudly as to appear vulgar but loud enough to seem mightily pleased.

"Is there a hotel in this fair city?" Will asked with a wink of his eye.

The girl laughed at his using such a description of the sorry little bump in the road which was her hometown. She shook her head.

"A local inn? A rooming house?"

"There's a shed beyond the house. It's a place where the hired men sleep during harvest time."

"Is it yours? I mean your daddy's?"

"No. It belongs to the town, if it belongs to anybody."

She smiled again and Will admired her little teeth, her clear, white skin. He reckoned her to be about seventeen.

A screen door slammed and Will turned to see a woman standing on the front porch, drying her hands upon an apron.

"Evalina," she called, and then again, "Evalina, ask those folks to come out of that hot sun onto the porch in the shade."

"Yes, Mama," Evelina said quickly, and turned to make the invitation she hadn't offered herself.

She forgot her manners, Will thought, when she laid her eyes on me. Will took it as a sign.

Paulette was seated on the porch swing, took up all of it. Mrs. Demming sat in the rocking chair fanning herself with her apron and smiling in the most pleasant way. Neither she nor Evalina had, by word or gesture, indicated it was anything greatly unusual in their lives to be entertaining such remarkable strangers.

The ladies talked on about sewing, the weather, and small, social matters. And all the while, Will and Evalina kept bumping eyes. Pepino sat on the steps of the porch, his head against a pillar, eyes closed and acting quietly happy. The Colonel entered into the women's talk like the little charmer he was.

After an hour, a truck rattled into the backyard. The men stood to greet Mr. Demming, just back from his fields. He was as calmly friendly as his wife and daughter. Maybe his eyes raised a little at the sight of Paulette and the Midget but it was only the merest shadow of curiosity and secret pleasure. He invited them all to dinner.

They ate at a long trestle table and the summer bugs sang all around in the twilight making it a day of wonderful good fortune.

Oh, there'd be no problem for shelter, the Demmings said. The men could sleep in the field hands' shed, but they insisted that would never do for Paulette. They'd make up a bed for her on the summer porch. Paulette started to cry for the generosity being shown them and the kindness given her. The Demmings didn't seem embarrassed by her tears. They just smiled and accepted them as thanks.

When it grew dark, it was time for bed, which was the way farmers lived.

In the shed, as they lay down their blankets upon the straw mounded upon simple, wooden, slatted cots, Pepino remarked that it had been a long, very long, time since such generous, unquestioning hospitality had come their way.

"If all the people of this town are like the Demmings, I might just stay on," said Pepino.

Will was slicking his hair in a bit of mirror fixed to the shed wall.

"What are you about, Will?" the Colonel asked, with a touch of fear growing in his voice.

"It's summer and that's a wonderful time for young girls that are so restless they can't get to sleep."

"What the hell are you saying?" the Colonel almost shouted. "That child's like a fawn and just as innocent."

Will showed his grinning teeth. "You don't know how to read the looks of a woman. . . ."

The Midget stiffened with alarm at his words. "Woman? She's hardly grown. Don't spoil things, Will. This could be a resting place for a little while."

"Go to sleep, little man. We'll want to be helpful with the chores in the morning," Will said, and went out into the velvet, summer dark.

Whatever the plan of his seduction makes no matter. How Will got the girl to leave her bed and room and join him on the moonlit grass was probably no special secret. It was an adventurous time for Evalina. Not that she was daring Will to try more. She was neither tease nor temptress.

She was as innocent as John recognized her to be. Maybe that urged Will to go further than he might have gone with girls who kept saying no when they meant yes.

while, there seemed no hate against any of them for what Will had done.

Will said nothing during that period of healing. Once they were on the road again, he told them all, over and over again, that what he'd said was the truth. He'd never made a move to touch that girl except to brush a spider from her hair. "It's the truth. The truth, I tell you!"

No one believed him though they nodded their heads, and that seemed to make him first terribly angry, then sad, and, finally, bitter as alum.

For a long time after, particularly when he was fuzzy with drink, he would suddenly murmur, "I didn't do anything," and cup his mangled hand with his good one. And sometimes he hid his eyes to hide the sight of tears.

In any case, he'd worn the wolf's clothing too long, and, perhaps, that one time he was wrongly hanged for it.

four in the van knew they were in a race with a force would destroy them. They knew it from the trem- of the mountainside. They knew it from the sound of earth slides that echoed up from the valley below. knew it in the large sense.

in the moment-to-moment assessment of their hey were gratefully unaware. Because they did not hey were able to labor on, pulling out this box and e, clearing the space to freedom. Were they to w closely death ran upon their heels, they may

Maybe he got terribly roused by her naive misunderstanding of it all.

Whatever. The first the others knew that something was amiss in the night was when they heard Evalina's thin, high-pitched voice crying out in fear and shame. It wasn't a scream. More a cry of outrage and hurt.

The Colonel and Pepino ran out onto the grass of the backyard, already dressed, as if expecting or dreading such an incident. There they found Evalina in her nightdress and robe, standing with her back against a tree, her hand at the throat of her torn garment. Will was wiping a laugh, nervous and unfunny, from his mouth with a suddenly nervous hand. He whipped his head around at their approach.

"What the hell have you done, Will?" cried the Colonel.

"Why, nothing. Nothing at all. We were just standing under the tree, Evelina and me, talking. It's a hot night and . . . and . . ."

"What have you done, you damn fool?" Paulette called from the summer porch, in her soft but carrying voice.

He turned around as if to answer to the new accusation and went on with what he was trying to say.

"We were just talking and a spider fell out of the leaves onto her hair. I brushed it off and she screamed."

"At your hand on her?" Pepino asked.

"No, at the damned spider. I was brushing it off. She was afraid of the spider."

Mr. Demming was there all at once. He was in his nightshirt. He had a shotgun in his hands as though he were prepared to shoot a fox after his chickens. Indeed, the chickens in the coop were kicking up one hell of a fuss.

Will looked at the farmer standing there and went on talking faster. "She jerked away and my hand must have caught the neck of her nightdress. Now, that's all that happened and that's the truth."

Mrs. Demming wasn't with her husband. Will seemed to know that she had stayed with Paulette on the summer porch.

"I swear on my mother's grave that that's the truth," he said.

"Shall we ask Evalina?" Mr. Demming asked softly.

Will's eyes flickered. "Ask her. Ask her," he shouted.

"She'd say you spoke the truth."

"Then you believe me?"

"No. Evalina wouldn't want you hurt or punished."

"Now, wait. Who's talking about punishment? Who's threatening to do me an injury. I'm innocent, I tell you."

Mr. Demming raised the barrel of the gun a bit. Will felt sweat breaking out on his forehead.

"Evalina is a good and gentle girl," said Mr. Demming, "who would never bear witness against someone, even if that someone did her harm."

"It happened just the way I said it. It was just a spider! Just a spider, I tell you!" Will was beginning to panic.

"But I know that Evalina would never scream at a spider's touch. You couldn't know that. She's not the least afraid of any living creature."

"Well, now . . . ," Will started to say.

"Come along behind the shed, Mr. Carney," the farmer said, motioning with the gun.

Will wanted to refuse, to turn and run, but he looked at the shotgun, which never wavered, and went along.

Mr. Demming looked at the Colonel and Pepino. "The two of you can come along. We don't believe in secret justice."

They went behind the shed. There was a machine set upon the stumps of two trees. It was a makeshift chain saw fashioned from the guts and gears of an old Chevy. It was, judging from the sawdust round it, the place where logs were sawed to size for winter wood.

Mr. Demming got it started by touching an open lead to the poles of an old battery. The machine coughed, kicked over, and then roared into life, the gears meshing and clanging one on the other as the saw started spinning. Will stared at it with wide-eyed horror.

"Come here," the farmer said.

Will started to tremble, backing away. Fast as a striking rattler, the farmer reached out a long arm and caught Will's left wrist in his own big hand. He exerted pressure and quickly brought Will to his knees with his great strength. Will gasped in pain.

Mr. Demming changed his grip, catching Will's a high above the forearm, near the elbow. His hand w big it nearly circled Will's arm.

Grim-faced, he drew Will's hand toward the sav

"*No! No!* Don't cut my hand off!" Will screamed

It was all happening so quickly. Pepino and the just stood there. They wanted to stop it but the ol was a force of nature, an avenging prophet, an that justice was on his side paralyzed them.

He pulled Will closer, dragging his whole b few feet, and, without apparent anger, forc into the gears of the machine.

Will let out a scream loud enough to wa tains from their ancient rest. The gears m tearing muscle and bone, then the eng Demming let go of Will's arm, freeing it machine.

Will fell to the sawdust, fainting d flung out and the hand at the end of

Afterwards, Mrs. Demming nurse and bandaging it. They fed the e weeks while Will recovered, unti danger, his slight fever and small

The
that
bling
small
They
But
peril, t
know, t
that ba
know h

well have lost their courage and lain down and let death take them. But they had a dream that made them over, that lied just a tiny bit to them, just enough to give them the power of disguise. And each, sensing his or her own inner greatness, labored on, lives rising up strongly in the shadow of death.

As they moved the weight about, shifting goods and clearing the way, the balance of the truck upon the mountain was kept even. The forces at work were many and subtle.

Water still percolated through the body of the earth, stones moved and pebbles slid away to form new dams and pressures, vegetation gave up its hold upon the earth, the weight of accumulated sand and mud moved down against the wheels of the truck.

The light from the worklamp had been growing dimmer. Now it became a subtle thing. The battery was giving up the last of its charge.

It was dark again.

Paulette gave a little gasp.

"I think the tunnel's big enough for all of us," the Colonel said. "Never mind the light. First, we must take Serena out."

"Take Paulette first. She's been very good and she's afraid," Serena said.

"No, no," Paulette began, but before she could protest further the Colonel cut her off. "There's no question of first or favor here," he said. "Paulette has to stay where she is to hold the balance of the truck. We can't risk her moving from that spot first."

His words were met with silence. They had grown weary and numbed with their terror, until it had become almost a comfortable and sleepy thing. They had lost the means to react to it. Thus, fresh knowledge of the deadly hazard started up the entire process of fear once again.

"Help me, Pepino."

The Colonel and the Rubber Man lifted Serena between them in their arms as they had done so often during the night. Pepino, crouched double, moved backward through the tunnel, taking great care not to bump into the sides of the tunnel. In the dark, they did collide once, and a stack of crates threatened to topple over on them. Serena, sensing the disaster, cried out softly, like a mouse.

But they made it to the end of the truck.

"Oh, God, how clean the air smells," Pepino said.

They set Serena down. Pepino scrambled off the tailgate and turned to lift her in his arms. The truck shuddered, shifted an inch. They all gasped but the truck moved no farther. Pepino held Serena in his arms. His eyes met the Colonel's in the dim light of the moon. They laughed silently into each other's face as though laughing at death.

They wanted to shout and leap about in their gladness. They just might make it after all.

The Colonel turned around and faced the mouth of the tunnel again. "Come along, now, Paulette. Carefully. Carefully and slowly."

After a long while her voice came back. "I can't. I'm afraid."

"There's nothing to be afraid of except staying where you are. You must come out."

There was another wait that seemed too long before she spoke again. "I think I'm going to faint," Paulette called out weakly.

From somewhere high up on the mountain, the mountain gave up another piece of itself. Out here, in the clear air, the sound of it seemed far louder than it had from inside the van, though, strangely, far less threatening.

"Damn it. You come right on out of there," the Colonel cried out.

They could hear Paulette's soft sobs as she began to cry. She reacted swiftly to her own hurt feelings.

Pepino stood holding Serena and looking about as though looking for a place to set her down. There was nothing but mud and slick puddles of water.

"Take Serena from me," he said to the Colonel, "and I'll go back inside for Paulette."

"No." The Colonel straightened himself and then shivered, not from the cold but for the courage he was about to ask of himself. "I'll go get her. It's for me to do."

The midget went back into the belly of the truck that loomed as dark as that of Jonah's whale. The journey back through the tunnel of boxes seemed to go on forever. He despaired of ever coming to the end of it. When he did, he walked toward the sounds of soft weeping.

"I didn't mean for you to come back," Paulette said when he touched her hand.

"Did you ever doubt that I would? For don't we love you? Now, take my hand, my sweet one, and I will lead you down the garden path."

Their hands touched and they began to move.

"You in there. What's going on in there?" Will suddenly called out. "Where's the light? What have you done to the light?"

"Don't answer him," the Colonel whispered.

"You'd better say something, goddamit, or I'll rock this goddamn truck over the side with everybody in it."

The Colonel entered the tunnel, leading Paulette behind him. She moved with a certain ponderous delicacy, shuffling her feet so that the weight of her should not move heavily from side to side. The truck groaned and shifted beneath their feet.

"You hear me? You hear me? Where the hell are you? Have you gone off and left me? Answer me, damn you?"

Will cried, begging, cursing, shouting, pleading softly for someone to answer him.

Paulette and the Colonel moved toward the back of the truck and freedom. They listened in all their blood and bones for the protesting heaves of the truck. It groaned, it shifted like a dragon coming awake. There were screams of metal and the gratings of stone. Will's cries became louder.

They reached the tailgate. The truck trembled. The Colonel leaped down into the mud.

"Sit down on the edge of the tailgate, Paulette, then ease yourself down carefully."

Ponderously, slowly, the Fat Lady seated herself, no mean feat in itself. Her legs hung down off the tailgate. She heaved forward, sliding off, to land with a great splat in the soft, wet earth. It was a comical tumble, as her legs held her for a second, then betrayed her and she fell headlong, like a dying dinosaur. She looked up unhurt, with a smile on her face.

Suddenly, they all began to laugh, happily, crazily.

"We did it, didn't we, Colonel? We rescued our own selves." Pepino grinned like no philosopher of Romany inclination had ever grinned.

Serena laid her head against Pepino's chest. There was a smile in her heart but she was tired past belief. She seemed like a flower crushed between the pages of a book, dried and containing only a memory of life. She was a dream that had found the end of the rainbow and had no other place to go.

"I hear you out there," Will's voice came to them. "I hear you all laughing. You got out? Did you all get out?"

The Colonel looked at Pepino.

"Are you all safe? You are! You are! Answer me, damn you! Where are you?" Will's voice was like a knife cutting through the night.

There was a pause, a failing of strength of voice, a silence that fell on the mountain. In that sudden silence, they all experienced Will's sudden knowledge of his own isolation and abandonment.

"Oh no! No!" he cried out, in a voice of deepest despair and awful knowledge. "You're going to leave me here to die!"

With great effort, they all helped Paulette to her feet. As one, they turned and started off on the long journey away from the mountain that had once held their lives in the balance.

The Colonel paused. They all seemed to listen with him for further cries from Will Carney. There were none.

"There's a bright life ahead for us all," said Serena, having tasted a triumph of being that surged through them all. Will seemed to have no part in their greatness. Seemed.

"Well, we owe him nothing!" suddenly cried the Colonel, as if trying to convince himself as much as them. "He lied to us all the days we knew him, cheated us, used us, treated us badly in a hundred ways."

The wild elation of rescue and salvation, the triumph of impossible accomplishment seemed suddenly to be dying in them all. Serena felt the feeling slipping away into sorrow.

"Yes," said Pepino gently. "He did all those things, surely."

Paulette was near tears, though why, she could not quite say. "He often said cruel, hurtful things to me," she said, sensing a need somehow for all of them to remember the bad that Will had done them all.

Serena felt cold and empty. Her power seemed to have vanished with the last of her strength. Her tiny body cried for sleep, for release. Yet Will, for all that, was like a wild animal about to attack her, crouching just beneath the

surface of her mind. No sleep could ever cleanse her of
the stark, animalistic terror, that primal scream she
sensed in Will, back there in the cab of the truck.

Her mind said Will could not be saved, to try it would
surely kill them all. And more than anything, she wanted
them to live, now that they had all found themselves, that,
each in his way, had come into his own. Yes, life was
important now, they now loved it in the deepest, everlast-
ing way.

The despairing wish, to make death love them, had
vanished in one swift dangerous night.

"He hated us for being freaks. I think he did," said the
Colonel. "He abused us for what we were and are."

Serena cried, tears flowing across her white face.

Pepino looked back up the road they must travel to
escape.

"I guess we should go now. It would be best."

They all understood his meaning. They should get away
before they were forced to witness the last living moment
of Will Carney, before the truck tumbled over, taking Will
to certain death.

"We couldn't do anything, anyway," said Colonel John.
"We're just freaks. Maybe if we were . . ." He let the
thought trail off because he realized suddenly, as if he
remembered a dream, that he didn't believe what he said
nor did any of the others. They would never be *just* freaks;
after this night, they were fabulous creatures of legend,
and damn well proud of it.

"In his way, Will is as much a freak as we are," said
Pepino, stopping and turning to face the dark hulk of the
truck.

"He's one of us," said Paulette, crying unashamedly.

"It might work," began Colonel John hesitantly. "If you
all got up on the tailgate to counter balance it . . . well, I
might be able to crawl across the roof and smash through

the windshield with a crow bar and somehow ease him out onto the hood. . . ."

"Paulette said, "I think . . . think we could . . . maybe."

Pepino shrugged. "It's worth a try."

Serena smiled in the dark. "We could all surely die in the doing of it." But as she said it, she was proud of them. Her heart filled with wonder, for they were greater than any dream she could have built for them, greater in heart than any she had ever known.

Colonel John laughed. "It's well known. Freaks must stick together, come hell or high water and this"—he laughed again—"this is both."

As one, the Rubber Man, the Fat Girl, the Midget, and the Moon Child turned in their tracks and plodded back through the mud to the truck.

Paulette said it for them all, said the last true thing that wedded them in their new love of living, that moved them.

"No one should have to die all alone," she said.

And each of them dreamed and dreams never die.

About the author

Sovereign Falconer is a former actor, musician, and experienced painter. As a screenwriter he has been nominated for the Academy Award, and as a novelist he has been nominated for the American Book Award, the Edgar, the Nebula, and other awards abroad. His books are widely published in many countries.

Jorge Luis Borges and Salvador Dali have both done introductions for his books.

Much lauded in Europe, where he has had literary best-sellers, he remains relatively unknown in America. Very little is known about the author and he has never been photographed in America. Extensively interviewed in Europe in magazines, on European TV, and in print, he has yet to grant a single interview in America.

He divides his time between his homes in Carmel, Los Angeles, and Amsterdam.

Attempts to locate the author in recent years have met with no success.

He never appears in public, does not answer his mail except via his agent, and can seemingly not be reached by phone.

There is much speculation as to his actual identity but very little information is available.